Kirkus Reviews (March 15, 2013)

Nothing gives a boy moral superiority like being awkwardly aroused by the least popular girl in high school. Tyler's friends call him "jerk," "idiot," "dick" and "asshead." Could he possibly be that bad? Is it that much of a problem that he's been dating sweet Sydney Barrett for years while crushing hard on friendless Becky Webb, shunned by everyone else in school for being the town slut? In a narrative that interleaves exposition-heavy flashbacks with his present (wasted in the park, drunk on butterscotch-pudding shooters), Tyler describes the history of his relationship with Becky. Perhaps that should be his nonrelationship, because he has spent years being unkind to Sydney while gazing dreamily at Becky's tattoo from across the cafeteria. Tyler's tortured overtures to Becky would be more believably redemptive if he didn't share in his classmates' double standard of shaming, needing to find a reason for Becky's sexual activities before he can find her worthy. Tyler, apparently, deserves a medal for choosing not to have meaningless sex with a suffering friend; what a hero. If Becky actually were a manic pixie dream girl, there'd at least be some whimsy breaking up the dragging, self-centered, deeply unkind angst. (Fiction. 14-16)

manicpixiedreamgirl

also by tom leveen

Party
Zero

manicpixiedreamgirl

. . . . .

TOM LEVEEN

random house new york

Text copyright © 2013 by Tom Leveen
Jacket photographs clockwise from top left:
photograph of girl © ˜skye.gazer/Flickr/Getty Images;
photograph of hands © Elizabeth Fernández G. Photography/Flickr/Getty Images;
photograph of boy © Fuse/Getty Images;
photograph of lights © Joy Sale/Flickr/Getty Images

All rights reserved. Published in the United States by Random House Children's Books, a division of Random House, Inc., New York.

Random House and the colophon are registered trademarks of Random House, Inc.

Visit us on the Web! randomhouse.com/teens

Educators and librarians, for a variety of teaching tools, visit us at RHTeachersLibrarians.com

Library of Congress Cataloging-in-Publication Data
Leveen, Tom.
Manicpixiedreamgirl / Tom Leveen. — 1st ed.
p. cm.
Summary: Seventeen-year-old Tyler Darcy looks back on his first three years of high school and considers the significant events involving Becky, his elusive "dream girl" who may be more troubled than he is willing to acknowledge.
ISBN 978-0-375-87005-7 (trade) — ISBN 978-0-375-87060-6 (lib. bdg.) — ISBN 978-0-307-97576-8 (ebook) — ISBN 978-0-375-87021-7 (pbk.)
[1. Best friends—Fiction. 2. Friendship—Fiction. 3. Dating (Social customs)—Fiction. 4. High schools—Fiction. 5. Schools—Fiction. 6. Emotional problems—Fiction. 7. Authorship—Fiction.] I. Title. II. Title: Manic pixie dream girl.
PZ7.L57235Man 2013 [Fic]—dc23   2012027694

Printed in the United States of America

10 9 8 7 6 5 4 3 2 1

First Edition

For Joy,
who I have loved
my entire life

manicpixiedreamgirl

one

· · · · ·

It's about a girl.

This isn't going to end well. Justin is curled up on the grass, on his back like a beetle, biting his thumb, laughing so hard he can't breathe. We've been drinking Western Flower champagne out of red Solo cups. Full red Solo cups.

Justin also concocted butterscotch pudding shooters. That'll look nice on the return trip, if you know what I mean. Robby and I abstained. Which probably helps explain why my head feels a bit lighter than my body but I still know things like my phone number, address, and gender. Robby, I think, is in about the same condition. Justin is . . . not.

Usually we don't drink at all. A celebration is in order, sure, but with the champagne bubbling in my guts, I'm starting to think a night of video games and pizza might've been a better idea.

"Someday," Robby says slowly, studying the rim of his cup, "I want to be just like you, Ty. I want to tell a story."

"You should," I say. "Writing is fun." Which, even as I say it, I know is one of the dorkier things I've ever said. And I've said a lot of dorky things. I keep a list. "Splendid abdominals" comes to mind. Also "milky belly."

"But I want to tell a *true* story," Robby says. "I want to be able to tell a story that ends with the sentence, 'And that's when the profound tsunami of blow jobs started.'"

Justin hacks, coughs, stutters a breath, and keeps laughing.

I force myself to laugh with him. My story *is* true—except for the whole "fiction" thing. Maybe "science fiction" is a better term, because my plot is about as realistic as a B movie.

"When do we get to read it, anyway?" Robby asks, taking a drink.

"Sometime," I say. "Listen, can I ask you guys something?"

"The capital of Guam is Hagåtña," Justin says, giggling.

"G'head," Robby says, trying to find a serious face to put on.

So I ask, "Do you think I should just tell her?"

Robby groans. Justin stops laughing.

"Oh, *shit*, Tyler," Justin says. "Not again!"

2

Robby chugs the last half of his champagne in one mighty gulp. A *super big gulp,* you could say.

He belches. "Justin's right," he says. "It's time to move on, man. *'Time to git goin'. What lies ahead I have no way a' knowin'. . . .'"*

Singing Tom Petty. Badly. Isn't he dead? It's taken a couple years, but Robby—currently wearing a distressed Zeppelin T-shirt—has circled back to a classic-rock phase.

Justin, still on his back, raises a hand. "Wait a sec," he says. He turns his head to one side. A second later, a great glut of butterscotch and champagne rockets out of his mouth and onto the grass. The sight of it makes my stomach roller coaster.

"Okay, I'm back," Justin says. He grunts and sits up, crossing his legs and dangling his hands off his knees. "What were we talking about?"

"Never mind," I say, and finish my drink. The champagne carbonates my bloodstream and burns acid in my stomach. So this is why we don't drink very often.

"You can't back out now," Robby says to me. He sits on top of the concrete picnic table where we've decided to hold our little party, his feet on the bench. "This needs to be addressed. So? Let's do this. Are you trying to say she has *no idea?* Seriously? Let's start there."

I look aimlessly around the dark park, hoping someone will happen by and mug us.

Robby and Justin aren't her biggest fans, and I know this. I never should have even brought her up.

. . . . .

I met her the first day of freshman year. Three years ago.

Well . . . not so much "met" as "made brief eye contact." It was enough.

My first crush happened in eighth grade. A girl named Lily Rose. No joke, that was her name. I'd thought Lily was "cute."

Rebecca Webb eclipsed cute and went straight to being the sun that lit and warmed my world.

If I could be any more melodramatic about how she made me feel, believe me, I would. It's the best I can do.

Becky Webb stood in front of me in line in the cafeteria that first day. All us freshmen seemed to be trying too hard to look cool: bangs in faces, shoulders thrown back or curled forward, sharp scowls or wide puppy-dog eyes. You could tell the upperclassmen by the way they'd snicker and shake their heads at everyone else, and by the fact that they'd shoved their way to the front of the line, leaving us ninth graders to bring up the rear. Yeah, looking cool was a mathematical impossibility on our first day of high school.

But we tried anyway. We collectively scanned the entire smelly, damp room as if we didn't care in the least that no one cared in the least about *us*. As if any moment, a group of popular seniors would wave us over to their kingdom-table. I was just happy I'd found the cafeteria without getting lost.

Like me, Becky scanned the cafeteria, moving her head in slow circles as we shuffled forward to order our soggy lunches. Our lighthouse-like movements must've been in sync, because for the longest time, I didn't notice her. I mean, I saw a girl with iridescent blond hair trimmed short in back, long in front; this girl a little shorter than me, in denim cutoffs and a dark blue ringer T-shirt, but I didn't see her face. Not until that moment.

When I changed my scan to a faster tempo, just to mix it up a bit, our eyes met.

I'd like to say she smiled at me. She didn't. Not really; it was one of those toothless *Hey, how's it going? Don't answer because I don't really care* sort of half grins you give people when you want to be polite but not start a conversation.

My head locked in place on my neck, my eyes wide, taking in every detail of her face.

That was it. The beginning of the end.

She faced forward again after our brief contact. A tattoo, half-covered by her shirt, graced the smooth curve where her shoulder met her neck: a nautical star, blue and black. Big, too—three or four inches across. I liked it, but it surprised me. A collared shirt would cover her tat, but her ringer T didn't. She *wanted* people to see it. And I wanted to ask her why.

This adorable, serene, tattooed girl picked up a chicken salad and carton of milk while I blindly grabbed whatever crap du jour was flung at me by the hairy cafeteria ladies. A suave gentleman might have purchased her lunch as a way to break the ice. Since I was not then and am not now a suave gentleman, I instead almost spilled my swill on the cashier as I watched Becky walk to an empty table.

A friendless dork myself, I sat at a half-full table several yards away to study her, tasting nothing of my lunch and ignorant—mostly—of the glares I got from the muscular, mustachioed seniors whose table I'd invaded.

Becky methodically arranged her food, adding to it a box of animal crackers from a cobalt messenger bag slung over her shoulder. She'd safety-pinned a patch to the front, but I couldn't tell what it depicted—a band logo, I guessed. She dumped the cookies on her tray and appeared to organize them.

How? I wanted to know. *By species? Alphabetically?*

Becky nibbled at her salad while pulling a paperback book from her bag. *Night Shift,* by Stephen King.

If I wasn't in love with her before this, now my devotion became complete. *Night Shift* was the first Big-Boy Book I'd ever read, sometime in fifth grade. It was an older book too. Not many people even knew about it anymore.

When the bell rang ending lunch, I chose the trash can nearest Becky to throw away my remains. My path, of course, took me right past her. She seemed in no hurry to get to class. Despite years of story writing, I had no words to say to her; speaking and writing are two vastly different skills, it turns out. I walked right past without saying anything. Even "hi" would've been a good start, but nope.

I did, however, glance at her zoo of animal crackers. On one corner of the tray: fully developed, healthy monkeys, giraffes, zebras. On the opposite corner: mangled, snapped cookies.

She was only eating the broken ones.

•   •   •   •   •

Pretending for my sake it's the first time we've had this conversation, Robby says, "What do you think of Rebecca, Justin?"

Justin says, "Well—"

"Shut up, I'm talking!" Robby says.

This cracks them both up. Justin falls backward, coming within inches of plastering himself with his own rich, creamy butterscotch puke.

"Forget it," I tell them. "Forget I said anything."

"Aw, I'm sorry, girlfriend," Robby says. "C'mon, keep yer skirt on. I'm serious, Ty. She doesn't know? Three years, and she has no idea how you want to give her a bit of the old—"

"It's not about sex," I say before Robby can complete his sentence. It's for the best. I don't want to know how it ended.

My friends stare at me. Justin, perplexed. Robby, amused.

"Not exactly," I add. "I mean, it's not even about kissing Becky. Not that she's not beautiful. She is."

Robby nods. Justin drools.

"If she showed up naked at my bedroom door and

said, 'Let's go,' I wouldn't say no," I go on. "I'm not that honorable."

Justin notices his drool and wipes it off with the back of his hand. Robby still looks at me like I'm an idiot.

Even from that first day, my attraction to Becky Webb was something different, something unusual. I wanted to hold her, protect her, hug her. One recurring daydream involved me holding her tightly as she wept in my arms. I'd tell her everything would be okay—whatever "everything" it was that bothered her—and that I was there for her.

It's a sick dream, I know. Selfish. If she was crying, then she had been hurt.

So then, what—I required her pain to satisfy my sick lust? I mean, how jacked up is that?

. . . I'm not explaining this very well.

Thankfully, my cell rings. I pull it out of my hip pocket, fumble it for a second, then blink at the screen, trying to decipher the caller's identity. The champagne, swiped from Justin's dad's liquor cabinet, has drawn hazy smoke curtains over my vision.

When the haze clears, I tap the green button on my phone.

"Hey, what's up?"

"Who is it?" Robby demands, trying to bum-rush me but tangling his legs in Justin's and crashing to the ground instead.

I cover the receiver with my thumb. "Becky!" I spit at them. "So shut up."

My friends look at each other, then back at me, and leap.

I backpedal, trying to evade. No luck. They tumble into me, and Robby gets his hands on my phone. While Justin plows his weight into my middle to keep me pinned, Robby puts the phone up to his face and shouts, "Hey, *Raw*-becca! We were just talking about you!"

Crap.

· · · · ·

I didn't stalk her or anything. But when I saw her around school, I did take note of where she was coming from or where she was headed. Over the course of about a month, I pieced together her schedule freshman year: English, math, biology, lunch, drama, computer lab, French.

I didn't follow her. I paid attention, that's all. Maybe one week I'd be on my way to English and see her coming out a door in the same hallway. Maybe a few weeks later, sent on an errand to the office, I'd pass an open classroom and see her in the front row in French. That kind of thing. At one point I realized we passed each other every day at the same place at the same time: by the trophy case near the office, between second and third periods.

I did not talk to her. What if she hated my guts? What if she laughed in my face? Too risky. Plus, this was high school now; she had hundreds of guys to choose from. What did I have to offer? Zits, cowardice, and silence? *Aw yeah.* Cue my rockin' theme music.

· · · · ·

"Yeah, hey, it's Robby," Robby says into my phone while I struggle against Justin. "Robby. Robby. ROBBY! Damn, woman, what am I, deaf?"

"Shut *ugh*!" I grunt. Justin, giggling at Robby's joke, digs an elbow into my gut, cutting off my breath.

"We're just hanging out at the park, drinking a little," Robby says to Becky. "Maybe a lot. I don't remember. Guess that's a good sign, huh? Yeah, so what're you up to tonight?"

If my best friend drops dead right this second, I'll be totally okay with that.

•   •   •   •   •

About two weeks into freshman year, I climbed on the city bus after school as usual. Mom, Dad, and my sister, Gabrielle, cared not at all that the city bus was a cesspool. In fact, they seemed to enjoy that I had to get up so early to make it to a bus that got me to school on time, *and* catch a bus home that took twice as long as a car. "I had to do it too," Gabby had sung during breakfast on my first day. "Have a good one, *freshman*!"

The city bus idled in a pull-out just beyond the school parking lot. I didn't know Robby when I sat down in the seat next to him. It was one of the few empty seats available, and I didn't blame anyone else for not wanting to sit there. Robby had headphones on, and he used his thighs as a drum kit for whatever noise he was listening to. He sang all the parts: vocals, guitars, drums, the works, alternating one for another.

Sighing to myself, I sat gingerly on the blue upholstered seat. He didn't even turn.

"*'Fatality!—reality!—you await the final kaaaaaaaaaaa!'*"

I had no idea what the last word was, because his voice reached an impossible pitch. He stopped drumming his legs long enough to throw two heavy-metal devil horns with his hands, turned to face himself. He was his own crowd.

At least he was having a good time. I turned to look out the window so as not to bug this weird kid . . . and saw Becky standing on the sidewalk beside the parking lot.

I sat up straight and watched as a flashy gray SUV pulled up to where Becky stood. She didn't move. A full minute must've gone by, during which the weird kid beside me began singing another song. Finally, a woman got out of the driver's seat and walked around the back of the car toward Becky. I assumed it was her mom. The woman wore pristine workout clothes with a baseball hat, hair pulled through the back, in a way that made me think she got dressed up and wore makeup to go exercise.

The woman paced quickly over to Becky and grabbed her shoulders. Pleading? Apologizing? I couldn't tell.

"*'Trapped in purgatory!'*" the kid beside me sang. "*'Galactic all triple eye!'*"

Huh? I wasn't sure if those were the actual lyrics or if the kid had no idea what they really were. Well, whatever.

The woman gave Becky a quick kiss on the forehead, scooted back to the driver's side, and climbed in. Becky didn't move; *hadn't* moved, in fact, since I'd noticed her. After another few moments, she walked to the SUV and got in. I watched the SUV drive quickly out of the parking lot and head west away from school.

I almost yelped in shock when Robby whirled on me and thrust the headphones in my face.

"Dude!" he cried. "You gotta listen to this. Do it! Listen to the double bass, man, just *listen!*"

Shocked, I took the headphones from him and put them up to my ears while he scrolled to the beginning of another song. I didn't recognize it, and it was too heavy and fast for my taste.

"You hear it?" Robby said, practically into my mouth. "Hear that double bass going?" He demonstrated the effect vocally.

I shook my head. "Sorry, man, I—"

"Listen!" Robby insisted, and started the song over again. "Listen *deeper.* Further back. Underneath the guitar."

All I heard was noise, but with him vocalizing the particular sound he was talking about, I was able to finally pick it out. And he was right: it was pretty cool once I could hear it.

"Yeah, that's . . . cool," I said, trying to give the headphones back.

"No, no! Wait for the bridge!" Robby said. *"Nuh-nuh-nuh-NAH, nuh-nuh-NAH, nuh-nuh-NAH!"*

I started laughing because I couldn't help myself. This worried me, because generally speaking, people don't like to be laughed at. But Robby just laughed right along with me.

Eventually, he allowed me to give him the headphones back as he went on and on about the band's drummer. About halfway to my stop, he donned the phones again and resumed pounding out rhythms on his legs.

Robby and I both reached for the stop bell at the same time, about fifteen minutes later, and touched hands, which made us both jerk back and look embarrassed. You know how that goes. He ended up pressing the long yellow strip, and he followed me as I got up and walked off the bus.

When we both took a few steps in the same direction, Robby stopped and pulled the headphones off.

"Okay, so where are you going?" he demanded. "Because I don't want to be all walking right next to you."

I pointed in the direction of my street. "Pinetree," I said.

"Aw, man, I'm on Cottonwood," Robby said. "Well, I guess I'll be walking right next to you after all. Unless you can't keep up."

With that, he started walking up the street. And I fell into step beside him, mostly because I needed to ask one question.

"Where'd you go to school last year?"

"Mohave," Robby said. "You?"

"Navajo," I said. "That's weird. You live on Cottonwood? That's only three streets up from me."

Robby shrugged. "Districting, I guess."

Turned out he was right about that. Our districts just happened to separate a block from my house. We ended up talking all the way to my street, mostly about our surrounding neighborhood and how weird it was that we'd never run into each other until today.

The next day, I got to the bus stop a little later than I'd meant to, and there was Robby, wearing a Megadeth T-shirt and playing drums on his legs again. When he saw me coming down the street, he waved and gave me devil horns.

"Morning, sunshine!" he shouted toward me. "By the way, I'm Robby."

We've been friends ever since.

• • • • •

"Rob, dude, stop!" I plead, trying to shove Justin off me. But Justin just grinds another narrow elbow into my ribs, laughing the whole time.

"Tyler?" Robby says to Becky over my phone. "Tyler . . . Darcy? Yeah, he's here somewhere."

"Rob! Seriously!"

"Yeah, here he is. Oh, wait! We had a question for you."

"Rob, I swear to god . . ."

"Yeah, we were wondering . . . what's up with you two? I mean, why won't you go out with him? He's a good guy. Talented. Smart. Sexy as all hell. Am I right?"

I punch Justin in the face.

• • • • •

I met Justin through Robby. They shared an earth science class, and had banded together at lunch. I'd been eating by myself, reading and also watching for Becky. One morning as we got off the bus, Robby told me to meet him in the cafeteria, and I agreed.

Justin sat reading a book at a table in the cafeteria, earphones plugged into an iPod. His face was screwed into a scowl as we walked up.

"Whatcha reading?" Robby said as we sat down.

"S'fer English," Justin said. "*The Glass . . . Ménage à Trois* or something."

"*Menagerie,*" I said.

"Hey, watch your mouth!" Robby said to me, and laughed at himself.

Justin and I hadn't so much as exchanged names at this point. He looked at me and said, "What're you, in Honors English or something?"

I was, but wasn't sure I should admit it. So Robby did it for me.

"Yeah, man, he's totally freaking brilliant!" he said. "Right, Ty?"

I didn't answer because I spotted Becky two tables down from us. Justin launched into a tirade about how stupid his English class was while I tried to figure out a way to get a better angle from which to see Becky.

"What're you listening to?" Robby asked Justin.

Justin took the earphones out and threw them at Robby. "Pink Floyd."

15

"Who's that? Any good?"

"No, they suck. That's why I'm listening to them," Justin said.

I barely heard Robby and Justin because I'd made up my mind: I would talk to that girl. I'd just walk up and introduce myself, ask her her name, and ask if I could join her for lunch. Maybe I could ask what she thought of *Night Shift*. Yeah! Perfect!

So I stood up with my lunch tray and ignored my thumping heartbeat as best I could. I took two steps—and stopped as some guy sat down right beside Becky.

I think my shoulders dropped all the way to the floor. Figures. The one time I grew a pair, and some dude got there before me. Older and bigger, too. Definitely a senior. I chucked my tray back on the table and sat down.

"Rough day at the office, sweetie?" Robby asked as he stuffed Justin's earphones into his head.

"It's nothing," I said, totally disgusted with myself.

"Ah," Justin said. "So it's a girl."

Whatever the look on my face was, it made the two of them bust up.

"Which one?" Justin asked me.

I tipped my head to the side. "Two tables down, on the end," I said. "Red-and-white baseball shirt."

"Oh yeah," Justin said, looking over at Becky. "I got her in math."

Justin became my newest, bestest buddy ever. "You do?" I said. "What's her name, what's she like?"

"Dunno," Justin said. "She doesn't talk much. Er . . . ever, actually, that I know of." He nodded appreciatively. "Cute, though."

"Do you know who she's talking to?"

"Mmm . . . nope. No idea. Parole officer?"

I did *not* think that was funny. Well—maybe sort of, but basically, no. The girl was an angel, anyone could see that.

"Dude!" Robby cried, with his hands cupped over his ears. "This song is . . . is rapture! This is like audio orgasm! Listen to this! Listen! Doesn't it just make you . . . wanna . . . *fuck* a guitar?"

He was so earnest that both Justin and I started laughing at him.

"What?" Robby asked, looking genuinely surprised.

"Can you even hear yourself?" I said, while trying to maintain a covert eye on Becky and figure out at least what grade the guy beside her might be in.

"I hear plenty," Robby said. "You filthy bitch."

Which made all three of us laugh even more. And by the time we'd finished, Becky and the guy who'd sat beside her were gone.

Of course, I didn't know that was her name then. Despite Justin having a class with her, I didn't actually learn Becky's name until I met Sydney.

You'll see the irony momentarily.

My English teacher, Ms. Hochhalter, ruled her classroom with an iron fist wrapped in unicorn stickers and glitter: Do what she says, you get along fine. Cross her, and you're done. Rumor had it she was into Roller Derby and stuff like that, which I largely think was BS.

That day, the same day I met Justin, Ms. Hochhalter stood in front of her desk waving a handful of papers at us as soon as the bell rang.

"Of all these autobiographical essays," she said, glaring at us, "only the barest handful are worthy of being written by students in my classroom. Sydney Barrett?"

On the far side of the room, a girl with thick, dark, springy hair raised her hand. "Here!" she said.

"A," Ms. Hochhalter said, flipping the essay at the girl, who yelped and caught it in one hand. "Tyler Darcy?"

"Here?" I said.

"A," Ms. Hochhalter said, throwing my essay at me. I did not catch it, despite a heroic effort. Sydney Barrett *watched* me not catch it.

"Teena Fortenbaugh?" Ms. Hochhalter went on, and called out only two other names of people who'd gotten As. I tried to hide behind my desk as the rest of the class growled at us. Honors English got a little competitive, I'd noticed.

"The rest of these papers?" the teacher said. "Sad, lonely, pathetic, heartbreaking. I'd sooner have chewed on a nice wad of tinfoil than grade these abominations." Ms. Hochhalter moved on to detail our next assignment, something about expository writing.

One of the cool things about her class was you could sit wherever you wanted, unless she moved you. The next day, Sydney Barrett sat down in the desk next to mine for the first time. I remember thinking there was something Greek about her, like she should've been lounging in a white marble colonnade in the first century. Her skin glowed pale olive, and something blazed magnetic in her eyes.

"Hi," she said, putting a hand out. "I'm Sydney."

"Uh . . . Tyler," I said, shaking her hand.

"My fellow A-getter," Sydney said, smiling. A nice, sweet, and confident smile. "We should form a club. You can be president if you want."

"I'm not too political," I said.

"Then I'll be president and you can be treasurer," Sydney announced. And smiled again.

The girl operated like a charming semitrailer, bulldozing her way through the world. It was a bit overwhelming, to be honest. Not unlike hanging out with Robby and Justin, actually, but like them, something about her fire-on-all-thrusters attitude impressed me.

As Ms. Hochhalter started class, I thought, *What if I'd been that up front with that girl in the cafeteria on the first day?*

●　●　●　●　●

Justin howls and falls off me, rolling with the punch. I scramble unsteadily to my feet and lunge at Robby, who giggles and throws my phone up in the air as he dodges. Smart move on his part; instead of tackling Robby, I have to switch gears and reach for the phone before it hits the grass.

Miraculously, even after the alcohol, I'm able to pick the phone out of the air.

"Hello? Hello?"

". . . Tyler?"

Her voice. God, her voice. No matter how often I hear it, it always turns me on.

"Hey, Becky. What's up, what's going on?"

Justin and Robby are both on the ground, hysterical. Either Justin's drunkenness made him not feel my punch, or—more likely—it wasn't that hard a punch after all. Okay, maybe it was more of a face-shove.

"What was all that about?" Becky asks.

Something about her voice doesn't sound right. But I can't place it, either because of the champagne or wrestling with Justin.

"What was *what* all about?"

"What was Robby talking about? About us?"

I fire a kick into Robby's shoe, which makes him laugh harder. "Oh, I dunno," I say. "He's pretty hammered, is all."

"Oh . . ."

"So, yeah, hey, what's up?"

"I . . . are you busy?"

I clear my throat. "Well, not exactly, just hanging out, you know."

I hear Becky sniff. Then again.

My chest cinches tight at the sound.

She's been crying.

•   •   •   •   •

"So, are you seeing anyone?" Sydney asked me in early October freshman year. Up till that point, we'd mostly made small talk about movies, music, and the stories we read in English.

"Nah," I said, trying to make it sound like a choice on my part. "Not really."

"You don't sound too sure," Sydney said, and poked my shoulder. Neither of us had moved our seats, so we were beside one another; despite the freedom to sit anywhere, by now most of the class had settled into places they thought of as their own.

"There's somebody I'm kinda . . . thinking about," I said. An understatement of *modest* proportions. While I was having a good time hanging out with Justin and Robby at lunchtime and sometimes going over to Robby's after school to play video games with them, it was a bit hard to concentrate on anything they talked about during lunch.

"Oh yeah?" Sydney asked, but her tone lacked any hint of mining for hot gossip. "Who?"

"Actually, I don't know. I haven't exactly talked to her. I don't know her name." Justin had kept promising he'd find out, but he never had. That, and he'd switched math classes. Much to my annoyance.

Sydney lowered her voice. "Is she in this class?"

"Nah, no."

"Oh." Sydney pulled the tie out from her ponytail, letting her dark hair drape over her shoulders. "Well then, what's she look like?" she asked, twirling a curl of hair in her fingers. "Maybe I know her."

"Um . . . well, she has this star tattoo on her neck—"

"Rebecca Webb."

Sydney, whether she knew it or not, was now my most priceless ally. I sat up straight, eyes popping. "You know her?"

"Yeah, we're in Drama One together."

I didn't know where to begin with my questions, and Ms. Hochhalter chose that moment to show up and start organizing her books on her desk. I had maybe thirty seconds.

"Well, what does she—is she like—how does she—you know!"

Sydney smirked at me and rolled her eyes. "Wow, you are hopeless, Ty," she said, and poked my shoulder again.

Ms. Hochhalter cleared her throat and opened a massive tome with gilt edges.

"What's she like?" I managed to spit out.

Sydney thought about it for a second before saying, "She's quiet."

The bell rang. "All right, my academicians, mouths closed, ears open," Ms. Hochhalter said. "We're starting Shakespeare today. I hear one groan, I see one adolescent eye roll, and your paper will be ten pages instead of five, plus you'll wash my car every week for the remainder of the year. Any takers?"

I loved having Ms. Hochhalter for English, but right then, I wanted her to shut up. This was important, couldn't she see that?

It didn't matter. Sydney faced forward and dutifully opened her notebook. I did the same while my veins throbbed impatiently for more details, and Rebecca's name whispered through my brain, echoing. I thought I could taste it.

"*A Midsummer Night's Dream*," Ms. Hochhalter said, taking a seat on top of her desk and crossing her ankles. "One of Shakespeare's great romantic comedies. Yes, children, the rom-com has existed for centuries. Usually we'd do *Macbeth*, which is much more macabre, but the drama department is putting on *Midsummer* as the fall play, so we'll all go to see the matinee together as a class."

Some kid in the back groaned. Ms. Hochhalter, without even looking at him, pointed in his direction and shouted, "My car, every week, rest of the year!"

While the class laughed, Sydney slipped me a note. *She's in the show.*

I wrote, *Ms. H?* and slipped it back. Sydney shook her head at me, wrote, and passed the note again.

Rebecca Webb is in Midsummer.

I didn't exactly adore Shakespeare, but I became an instant convert to the Bard. And English class would never be the same. In more ways than one, it would turn out.

The following week, I passed Becky in the hall on my way to math, like I did every day. I'd memorized her motions—the way she kept a book clasped in both arms in front of her chest, the way her left hip twisted just a bit more than her right with each step, the bounce of her cobalt bag against her thigh. The patch on her bag read *Just This Once* in white courier font. Yeah, try narrowing down *those* words in Google. I had no idea who or what it referred to.

And on this particular day, Becky looked right at me.

No mistaking it. Not only did we make eye contact, but she maintained it. Studying. Forehead wrinkled ever so slightly. Kept my gaze until we'd passed.

I stopped and turned, to see if she'd look back at me. She didn't. It could have been coincidental; maybe I'd just happened to fall into her line of sight? But no, she hadn't *glanced,* she'd watched me. Which meant . . . !

Then a senior guy banged into me and sent me to the floor. I had enough pride to be embarrassed as laughs and applause echoed up and down the hall, but not so much as to distract me from watching Becky walking away. She was too far by that point to have seen my little spill. Good.

Recovering, I shoved the guy who'd crashed into me and called him a dick.

"Oh yeah?" he said. He stood eight feet taller than me. "You think so, freshman?" He dropped his backpack to the floor and pushed me with one hand, sending me back about three hundred yards into the wall.

Three of his senior buddies circled me, lowering their square heads and sharpening their razor teeth. Freshman year was about to get a lot shorter. My last thought on Earth was I'd never get to see Rebecca Webb in *Midsummer.*

"Three against one?" I heard Robby shout. "That's not

even *remotely* pussy!" He and Justin appeared behind the seniors, who whirled toward them.

"Hey!" some random teacher shouted. "That's enough. Get to class!"

The seniors melted into the crowd with lifted middle fingers and scowls. Robby and Justin came up to me.

"Were you going to fight them?" I asked Robby as my heart rate struggled to return to normal.

Robby gave me a shocked expression. "Aw, *hell* no," he said. "I was just buying time for someone to break it up."

I couldn't help laughing, and neither could Robby and Justin. We went on to our classes. I've considered them both my best friends from that day on.

I checked to see if Becky had witnessed any of this, but she wasn't in the hall anymore. And while I should've been scared for my life, mostly I couldn't stop thinking about the look she gave me.

Rebecca Webb knew I existed.

·   ·   ·   •   •

I can feel my eyebrows crashing together as I frown at the near-sob in Becky's voice. Something—or someone— hurt her.

"Becky?"

"I was, um . . . ," Becky says, then stops. I hear her take a shuddering breath before she goes on. "Is there any chance maybe I could get you to come over for a while? Just for a bit?"

"Yes," I say. "Of course, yeah, absolutely. I'm on my way, okay? All right?"

"Thanks, Ty," Becky says.

"Be there soon," I say, and hang up.

Robby glares at me.

"I gotta go," I tell them.

"You aren't going *nowhere,* brother," Robby says.

I can't tell if he's swaying or I am. "Dude, something's wrong with Becky, I gotta go see her."

Justin stands up beside Robby, blocking my path to the parking lot. Robby shakes his head.

"Not like that, bro," Robby says. "Uh-uh."

"What?"

"Dude, you're wrecked," Robby informs me. "You're not getting in that car."

"Screw you," I say. "I barely had half what you did, and—whatever. Becky needs me."

I take a step toward the parking lot. Robby sidesteps to intercept.

"Ty," he says, "you take one more step toward that car, I'm gonna punch you in the dick."

·　·　·　·　·

Robby was only a skinny little dweeb freshman like me that day he and Justin interfered with my imminent senior beating. Since then, he'd put on about twenty pounds, maybe more, most of it muscle, and he'd grown about six inches. Growth spurt, I guess. I'd gotten taller, but

26

not much else. No matter his size, one thing was still true about Robby Jackson: he was no bully, and he wasn't violent, but he also wasn't afraid of anyone.

Least of all me.

Robby was one of those laid-back, easygoing, funny, and fun-loving types who can and does get along with virtually everyone. Pick any high school label you want—Robby had friends who fit it. Probably that's because during freshman and sophomore years, he raced through pretty much every style of clothes and music known to man. By the third month of freshman year, he was wearing nothing but basketball shorts and jerseys while he listened to rap and hip-hop, his heavy-metal T-shirts forgotten. Later it was all black shoes, white socks, and nothing but Johnny Cash and rockabilly. And wherever Robby wandered, he left a trail of charmed friends behind.

Well, no. Not friends. Not the way he would define it.

Justin and I went with Robby's parents on a day-hike trip toward the end of freshman year, before the summer weather really hit. I remember sitting after a three-hour hike, tired, sore, and out of breath. Exhilarated, though, because the view from this mountaintop was awesome.

"Thanks for coming with me, guys," Robby said suddenly as he gazed at the panorama around us.

Justin and I traded a glance. It wasn't the kind of thing a fifteen-year-old guy goes around saying. But then, that was Robby. Spoke his mind, consequences be damned. I always respected that about him.

"Uh, sure," I said, and Justin gave some kind of affirmative sound as well.

"Nobody else would've gotten it," Robby went on.

"Gotten what?" I asked.

But Robby just shrugged and grinned. He broke out bottles of water from his pack and passed them to us. Justin and I had drained ours half an hour before.

Justin brought up plans for the summer. We talked about that for a while, while I tried not to have a panic attack at the thought of not seeing Becky for three months solid.

On the way back down the mountain, as Justin lagged behind, I asked Robby, "What did you mean about getting it?"

"Ty," he said, "you ever notice I know a lot of people at school?"

I said I had.

"But I wouldn't climb a mountain with 'em," Robby said. "That's all."

•   •   •   •   •

"Get out of my way, Rob."

"No, sir."

I consider trying to make an end run around him. It won't work. He's too fast.

I try whining instead. "Come on, man!"

"Text her back, tell her you can be there in a couple hours," Robby says. "Because seriously, you're not driving before then."

Still pissed, but somehow managing to grasp the wisdom in what he's saying, I text Becky.

Need couple hours. Can't drive. Cool?

The three of us wander back to the concrete table, and before I even sit down, she's texted me back.

NVM thx.

"Oh, god*dammit!*" I show Robby the screen. "See that? Thanks, asshole."

"That's me, the asshole keeping your drunk ass alive," Robby says, faking sorrow. "Tough luck, compadre."

"I'm not drunk!" I say.

Justin picks up the champagne bottle. "Drink?"

My cell buzzes. Thrilled, I check it, assuming it'll be Becky, changing her mind.

"Ah, shit."

"What's up?" Robby asks.

"Nothing," I tell him. "It's Sydney."

two

· · · · ·

After that day in the hall when Becky looked at me, the tables turned. Now it was Becky keeping an eye on *me*. At first I liked it. I mean, why wouldn't I, right?

But she never said anything! Of course, neither did I. I couldn't figure out why she'd suddenly gained interest in me. We had no classes together or anything like that. Which, honestly, was another mystery; our high school was pretty big, but you'd think our paths would cross in some class or another.

I'd spend pretty much every night pacing my room, developing mental movie scripts to talk to her in a variety of smooth, cool, charming ways.

FADE IN:

INTERIOR. SCHOOL HALLWAY.

TYLER DARCY, cutting an ironically dashing figure in jeans and a tight T-shirt that shows off his splendid abdominals, leans back casually against a wall. Two—no, four!—seniors walk past him and cower when Tyler gives them the slightest sneer of disregard.

From around the corner enters REBECCA WEBB, an adorable girl with blond hair like corn silk, blossom skin, and the slightest wry tilt to her hips. Her perfectly shaped rear is cupped not too tightly and not too loosely in blue jeans. She eyes Tyler, who kicks off the wall and saunters to meet her. The other students move to walk around, many of them casting glances of envy at Tyler's good fortune.

                    REBECCA
So, I know we haven't ever really talked before, but—

> TYLER

—you were thinking we should go out for coffee and get acquainted.

> REBECCA (smiling shyly)

How did you know?

> TYLER

You can't fight fate, Rebecca.

> REBECCA

You know who I am?

> TYLER (caressing her cheek)

I've always known.

Slow dolly forward as he tilts his head to meet her lips. This kiss is so exquisite, so beautiful, that the other students dissolve away into . . . No, wait, they stop and watch, in total awe of their perfection. FADE TO BLACK as Bob Dylan's "Can't Help Falling in Love" plays under.

A real Oscar winner, right?

In these scripts, she was demure yet possessing a great sense of humor. She was smart, but impressed by my own natural brilliance. That kind of thing. You know how it goes.

Luckily, I never wrote any of that down.

I don't know if our drama department was anything outstanding or not, but the production of *A Midsummer Night's Dream* was pretty good. I think Becky was supposed to be a fairy or a sprite or something, named Mustardseed, but the director had gone all conceptual and reimagined the play in the 1930s, so everyone was playing old-time movie actors, like W. C. Fields and the Marx Brothers.

I'm not saying the show was good just because Becky was in it. It helped, most likely, yes, but she wasn't the only reason. I liked it because William Shakespeare definitely felt my pain.

I am beloved of beauteous Hermia; the course of true love never did run smooth—page after page of stuff like that, things that if you said them out loud, for real, would get your ass rightly kicked, but when Shakespeare says it . . . I dunno, man.

Then there was Becky herself.

I didn't know this at the time, but thanks to Ms. Hochhalter—like it or not—I found out Shakespeare used two forms of writing in his plays: prose and verse. Typically, royal characters use verse, which rhymes, and common characters use prose. The actors in *Midsummer* who spoke in verse generally got monotonous, like they were really bad rappers or something. A few were pretty good. One of those few was Becky Webb.

When she spoke the poetry, I swear her entire body lit up. Maybe it was makeup or something, but her eyes seemed to sparkle and her face to shine. I felt myself leaning forward whenever Becky danced onstage. Her first scene, opposite the main fairy, Puck, was short and sweet, but immediately added to my imaginary biography of Becky, famous star of stage and screen. I thought maybe instead of movie scripts, I should be writing plays for her.

At one point in the play, the fairies did this dance, wearing old-fashioned tuxedos. Something about the way the top hat tilted on Becky's head, the playful smile she cast out at us in the audience—I saw the show only once, yet was sure I had the entire dance number memorized. The way she carried herself at school didn't do her body justice. It wasn't just the dance routine, it was the way she moved across the stage—glided, almost. I know I'm biased, but I swear she captivated the entire audience. I didn't miss a moment of her performance from my seat in the middle of the auditorium.

Right beside Sydney Barrett. Whether she'd planned it that way, or I had, or neither of us, I couldn't say.

When I wasn't mentally scripting epic films starring myself and Becky Webb, I continued using Sydney as my main source for anything Becky-related. Or, as was often the case, making a complete idiot of myself.

"What did you think of 'The Lottery'?" Sydney asked after we'd read the story in class before Thanksgiving break.

"Good," I said. "Creepy."

"Yeah," Sydney said. "I thought it would be a cool reader's theater piece."

"What's that?"

"Reader's theater? It's like a staged reading. Everyone has a script, it's not memorized. Usually you do it black box."

"You read it in a box?" I asked, imagining our drama club standing in empty brown shipping boxes.

Sydney laughed. When Sydney laughs, everyone notices, and I kind of liked that about her. She was fearless.

"No, 'black box' means you don't wear costumes or use props, and your only furniture is black wooden boxes, like crates or something. It just means, like, stripped down."

I'd like to see Rebecca stripped down, I thought, and laughed at my own stellar wit.

"What's so funny?" Sydney said.

"Nothing," I said. "So is that something you'd, like, do for drama class?"

"Yeah, maybe."

"You could ask Rebecca to help."

Yep. Really said that. I wish I could go back in time and punch myself in the kidney. Way to go, fifteen-year-old me.

Sydney's eyebrows pinched. "Rebecca Webb? Why?"

Caught in the open, I said, "I just mean, you know. Maybe she'd—she'd help out. Or something. Perform. Or whatever." I could see Sydney wasn't overly impressed with this idea, so I hurried to add, "I'd come see it if you did."

"You mean you'd come see it if Rebecca was in it?"

"No! I mean, I'd come see it anyway. If you did it. That's all."

Sydney laughed again, and patted my forearm. "You're sad, Tyler," she said, but left her hand on my arm for a few seconds. Her fingers were cool and soft.

I tried to avoid bringing Becky up in conversation after that, with mild success. I assume Sydney didn't pursue her black box idea with "The Lottery," or if she did, I never heard anything about it.

On the last day of school before Christmas vacation, Sydney turned in her seat right as the bell rang ending class.

"So, have you talked to Becca yet?" she asked.

I said, "Who?" Sydney hadn't used the nickname Becca before.

"Rebecca Webb?" Sydney said. "The girl you've been slobbering over since September?"

"I wasn't slobbering!" I said. And thought, *At least, not literally.*

"Oh, okay," Sydney said. "Sorry. Have you?"

"Well! . . . Not exactly."

"You know I told her about you, right?"

I almost convulsed. "You did *what*? What did you say, what did *she* say, what—"

"I just told her you'd mentioned her," Syd said, seeming to enjoy my freak-out. "That's all."

That's why Becky had suddenly started noticing me. I

didn't know whether to be happy or mad about it: happy that Syd had sort of opened the door, but mad that Becky hadn't noticed me just because of *me*.

"Oh," I said. "Okay. But what did she say?"

"Nothing. Literally. I'm not even sure she heard me."

She did, I thought. *Yes, she did.*

"So anyway, what're you doing tomorrow night?" Syd asked.

My entire body lit up. This could only mean one thing: Becky had asked Sydney to ask me if I was busy, in preparation for asking me out.

"Nothing!" I said. But I sounded desperate, so I added, "I mean, writing, I guess."

Syd made a mock-disgusted face. *"Homework?* Really? I know I'm all brainy and junk, but even I don't do homework over Christmas." She nudged my arm.

"Nah, no," I said. "I mean a story."

"Oh. Like, for fun?"

"Uh, something like that," I said. Classes were trading places by then, and the next class was seniors. I didn't want to get caught in there with them if I didn't have to.

Nor did I feel like explaining my writing. Not many people knew about it back then. Robby, Justin. My parents and Gabrielle, I guess. That was it. I'd pretty much plagiarized my first short story in fifth grade, a rip-off of one of the short stories in *Night Shift,* in fact. Changed the character names and some dialogue and small parts of the plot. It was how I learned. I didn't think I was good enough to actually show anyone what I was writing, despite being in Honors English and getting As on my writing assignments.

Sydney stood up when I did. "Well, we should hang out tomorrow," she said, as if out of the darkness of time and space. "See a movie or something. Wanna?"

At first I deflated, seriously bummed Syd wasn't asking me about my plans on Becky's behalf. But Sydney and I did have fun talking in class, even if half our conversations revolved around me trying to learn more about Becky. Sydney was confident, had that big brassy laugh . . . her hair was really pretty awesome . . .

"Um, yeah," I said. "Sure. I guess so."

"Great!" Syd grabbed my arm and wrote a number down on my palm.

"Call me, or text or something," she said, like she did this sort of thing every day. My god, if I'd tried this same approach with Becky, I'd have asphyxiated from my own stupidity.

"Yeah, okay . . ."

"Cool. See you tomorrow, then!"

She picked up her bag and zipped out of the classroom before I could think to say anything else. Like, for instance, *What the hell did I just do?*

Sydney was cute, but . . . *Lily Rose* cute. However, since I lacked the testicular fortitude to make contact with Becky, I went ahead and called Sydney the next afternoon and met her at the mall that night. We saw some dumb comedy, and I don't even remember which one, a fact she will be happy to repeat any old time, thanks much.

After that, we got Panda Express in the food court. Syd ordered a full meal. "Know what I hate?" she asked as we found a table.

"What?" Now that the movie was over and we were moving on to the actual talking part of the evening, I wasn't sure I'd be able to keep up with her.

"Girls who won't eat," Sydney said, which made me laugh. Syd jabbed a fork into her noodles, grinning. "Seriously! I mean girls who won't eat in front of guys. Who're all, 'Just a salad and a cracker for me!' or whatever, and then go home and binge on Zingers and Pepsi."

Becky was partial to salads, I'd noticed. I didn't point it out.

"Thanks for dinner, by the way," Sydney added.

"No problem," I said, and watched her eat while I fiddled around with my own meal. After the way she said all that, I half expected her to eat like a front loader, but she ate thoughtfully, taking her time and maybe savoring each bite.

I made sure to keep my mouth closed when I chewed. That's about as high a bar as I could set at that point. Also, I might've stretched a little on the "no problem" paying for dinner part; between dinner and the movie, I was tapped for the week. But I didn't mind.

We talked about school and parents and siblings and whatnot. We marveled that both our sets of parents were still married, agreed Ms. Hochhalter walked on water because she assigned good stories and occasionally cussed in class, and decided that Gabrielle and Syd's older brother would make a terrible couple.

Becky's name did not come up. At least, not out loud. Mentally, I couldn't help but make comparisons.

Take their styles, for instance. Becky wasn't a slob or anything, but she did seem to trend more toward basic T-shirts, shorts, and scuffed jeans. Syd, then as now, always looked more put together. She seemed to favor fashionable sweaters—cardigans, I think they're called—and dark jeans that looked like they'd been tailored to fit her. Her clothes were generally bright and bold, her fingernails painted brilliant colors. She came off looking like a junior or senior instead of a lowly freshman.

I couldn't say which I liked better. They both fit.

The worst thing about freshman year was no one had a car except parents and older siblings. Mom had dropped me off, and I was supposed to call Gabby to pick me up. Which, essentially, sucked. But what was true for me was true for others: if you had no car and didn't want to be home, there were only so many options.

So I should've guessed that since we were now officially on winter break and it was a Friday night, there was a good chance we'd run into someone we knew from school. Some-one turned out to be someones, namely Robby and Justin and the girls they were dating at the time.

40

"Hey!" Robby called in his usual boisterous voice. "Tyler! What's up?"

"Hey," I said as the four of them gathered around our table. The two girls, their names long since lost to history, crowded too close to the guys, texting furiously. I wondered if maybe they were texting each other so they wouldn't actually have to speak.

Before I could say anything beyond my greeting, Robby stuck a hand in front of Sydney's face. "I'm Robby," he announced.

Sydney didn't rush to finish chewing and swallowing her bite of food. "Syd Barrett," she said, reaching across her body to shake Robby's hand.

Robby goggled his eyes and stared at her. "*The* Syd Barrett?" he asked, shaking her hand.

Justin said, "Awwww, sweet!"

Robby said, "Wow. I was expecting someone older. And male. And British."

"It's short for Sydney," she said, not the least bit put off. "With a y."

"Oh, I'm sure." Robby grinned at her, and when she wasn't looking, tossed me a backward nod, like I was supposed to get the joke. I didn't, not then. He explained it to me later.

"What're you guys doing?" Justin asked, directing his question mostly at me while sliding curious glances at Syd.

"Uh . . . just . . . eating," I said.

Justin contorted his face. "Wait a sec," he said. "She's not the girl who you—"

"Dude!" Robby cried. "I almost forgot! We gotta get tickets for the Executives show next weekend. Right? You're going, right?"

"Um . . . the who?" I said while avoiding Sydney's smirk. Robby's derailment of Justin was not among the most subtle.

"Never mind, we'll fix it up later," Robby said. "You two kiddies have a good time."

"Yeah, see ya," Justin said, scowling at Robby and clearly having no idea what had just happened.

Their two girls didn't say a word, their heads still tilted down to watch their phones. They were somehow able to navigate completely blind this way, like they had echolocation apps.

"Bye," Sydney said, waving. Robby waved back for all of them, and then they were lost in the mall shuffle.

"The Executives are a band," Sydney told me as she turned back to her food. "You're going to the show?"

"I guess so," I said. The name sounded familiar, like they were a band Robby had mentioned before, but I didn't know anything about them.

Sydney shrugged and twirled lo mein on her black plastic fork. "Well, that would be cool," she said.

She didn't bring up Becky. And I was glad. No—relieved.

After eating, we went outside to wait for her dad to pick her up. A low concrete wall divided the sidewalk from the mall landscaping, and Sydney sat down on it, throwing one leg over the side like she was getting on a horse.

I couldn't explain it then, and I don't think I can now, but something about that simple move made me see Syd a little differently than I had the day before in English. It wasn't a feminine thing to do, really, but she did it with a sort of grace. Or maybe it was ease; somehow, that gesture told the world she was completely at home with herself.

I don't know.

I sat down beside her. Syd put both hands in front of her and leaned forward on them.

"So, listen," she said, "are you going to talk to her at some point?"

Because I'm a dumbass, the first word out of my mouth was, "Who?"

Syd rolled her eyes, but smiled when she did it. "Tyler . . . ," she said.

I looked at the sidewalk. "Honestly?" I said. "Probably not." That was the truth of the thing. Rebecca Webb was too . . . too *everything* for a troglodyte like me to ever think of approaching. I think even her tattoo intimidated me. Sometimes when I thought about her—you know—she wore her costume from *Midsummer*. It had fit her very nicely, that's all I'm saying.

Just a few days before, Justin and Robby and I'd had a conversation about what celebrities we wanted to meet someday, and which ones would make us—to quote Robby—"lose our shit" if we did meet them. Robby had listed off a whole ream of musicians and bands. Justin said Gracie Cee, some famous female soccer player I'd never heard of.

I'd said Stephen King, primarily because I did not want to say Rebecca Webb. If losing one's shit was the standard we were going to use, I was sure I'd lose mine if I did talk to her.

"Really?" Sydney said, leaning a little closer. "You really don't think you'll talk to her?"

"Kinda doubt it," I said.

"Hmm," Syd said. "Cool."

Her dad arrived in this enormous black four-wheel drive and stopped next to the sidewalk. Sydney said, "That's my ride. Call me later if you want."

And leaned over and kissed me, once, quick, on the lips. In front of her dad and everything.

I sat there for another twenty minutes trying to figure out what had just happened before walking home, completely forgetting that my sister was supposed to pick me up.

I called Sydney the next day.

That was it. The beginning of the end.

Two years ago.

three

• • • • •

I hit a button on my cell as Robby, Justin, and I sit at the concrete table again.

Sydney's text reads: *Where are you?*

Two years, remember. More than two. Good god, it's already May.

I write back: *At park with Robby and Justin.*

Sydney: *Who else would it be? What are you doing there?*

I shut my eyes, start to tip over, open them again quickly. I shove my phone back into my pocket. I don't feel like dealing with Syd right now.

"What's up?" Justin asks me. His eyelids are drooping, his mouth hanging slightly ajar.

"She just wants to know where I am," I say.

"You should really get those back someday," Robby says.

"Get what back?"

"Your *balls*."

"But they match her purse!" Justin says, and cackles.

"Dude—" I start saying to Robby, but my phone rings. Not vibrates; it's a call.

Snorting, I pull my phone back out and check the ID. Yep.

"Yeah?" I say after tapping the call button.

"What're you doing at a park?" Syd asks.

"Hanging out."

"You mean just sitting there?"

I stand up and walk away from the table with my friends watching me. Justin's still enthralled with his own drunken humor while Robby's giving me the stink eye.

"Yeah, pretty much, just sitting here."

Silence.

"What?" I ask.

"Nothing," Sydney says, which is another word for "something."

"Syd, what?"

"You sound drunk. Are you drunk?"

"Maybe a bit." But I don't think I'm so far gone as drunk. Tipsy, maybe.

"Jesus, Tyler, are you driving?"

"Through the park? No. Not quite that far in the tank."

"You know what I mean."

46

"No, Syd. Robby won't let me."

"So you were *going* to."

Maybe because I *am* tipsy, or maybe because I want to set her off, I say, "I was going to go help Becky with something, but Rob said no because I was drinking."

Silence.

Penetrating, unending silence. Silence with brilliant crimson fingernails.

·   ·   ·   ·   ·

Somehow, by the time the second half of freshman year started up again after Christmas, Sydney and I were a couple. I couldn't tell you how. I called her, and she texted me, and I texted her, and we hung out, and we friended each other, and she called me, and we hung out again, and I texted her, and . . .

There was no discussion about it. No *Will you go out with me?* No romantic overtures or an exchange of high school vows. Neither one of our online romantic statuses changed. I'd searched and searched for Becky but had never found a Facebook or any other page for her—which was probably just as well, because I wouldn't likely have tried to friend her out of the blue anyway. Still, I kept my romantic status "single," just in case.

Which of course makes me an asshole. But remember, Sydney didn't change hers, either, so.

I couldn't understand why Syd would even want to go out with me in the first place. I mean, she must've known how bad I had it for Becky after hearing me talk about her—what little I knew—and asking her all kinds of questions about Becky prior to that first movie date.

Becky's name morphed into an unspoken topic hovering in the air between our words and our kissing. Yeah, I kissed Sydney. A lot. And more than *that* by summertime.

And through it all, I thought and wrote about Becky.

I'd started writing a story about her—about us—before Christmas break, and it was something I went back to again and again, polishing, revising, rewriting, reworking, trying to make it perfect.

I hoped someday to give it to her. Since I was apparently incapable of speaking, maybe my writing would win her over. I felt like it was all I had to offer. I was happy to note at the time that Becky didn't seem to have a boyfriend hanging around, and I lived in mortal terror of seeing her in the hall holding some guy's hand, or kissing someone in front of a classroom door before the bell. But I didn't see anything like that all during freshman year. She was always alone. The only time anyone sat with her was that once, the day I met Justin. And I never did see that guy around school. It would be a while before I solved that little mystery.

The summer before tenth grade was tough, because obviously there was no chance of seeing Becky. Sydney kept me occupied, for the most part, which was . . . nice. I guess. Neither of us went on vacation, so we got together probably twice, three times a week. The rest of the time I was either at home writing or out with the guys playing video games, throwing darts in Robby's basement, doing some mild trespassing on golf courses late at night, that kind of thing. Syd and I talked every night. That's what couples do, after all.

This thing with Syd . . . it just sort of happened. I guess it was a combination of her very forward nature and my utter lack of balls, despite what Robby thought had happened to them. Syd wasn't all demanding and needy, really. I don't expect any sympathy on this point, but the fact is, she was a good-looking girl who was also pretty smart—she had four more honors classes besides our English class—and she could hold a conversation. I liked those things about her.

And I liked hooking up with her. Not going to lie about that.

As August rolled around, I was initiating our make-outs as often as she was, because, I mean . . . well, it was there. I was fifteen, a guy, and here's a cute chick who likes hooking up with me. Maybe a better man could have called it off, but I wasn't a better man.

I think for those first few months together freshman year, it would be fair to say I was tolerating Sydney. By the end of summer, though, it was more like: lust plus fun minus access to Becky equals . . . keep dating Sydney.

I never said "I love you" to Sydney, and Syd didn't say it to me. I knew I didn't love her. And maybe somewhere deep down, she knew she didn't love me, either. And we both knew the other knew it. That's what I told myself, anyway.

On the last night of summer vacation before tenth grade, Becky's name finally came up in conversation.

"Ty," Sydney said, lying next to me on the floor of my room after we'd been making out for about an hour while Mom was shopping, Gabby was at school, and Dad was at work, "we need to talk."

Part of me was relieved, assuming we were about to break up. It would be a bummer, no doubt, but I had other things on my mind. Like Becky. I'd get to see her the next day after a three-month dry spell. Since it was impossible to find someone named Becky Webb or Rebecca Webb online, all I'd been able to do over the summer was keep an eye out for her. Fat chance.

I still had a thousand scripts ready to try out on Becky, unwritten words I'd planned in my mind, except, of course, now I couldn't on account of Sydney. Many of my scripts included the Breakup Moment—the point in time where, as Becky fell hopelessly in love with me, I'd have to cut Syd loose.

I might've been an ass for yearning for Becky Webb while dating someone else, but I wouldn't cheat on Syd.

Plus, I mean . . . what were the chances Becky was going to fall for me anyway?

"It's about Rebecca," Syd said.

My stomach shriveled with guilt, as if Sydney somehow knew about the stories saved on my computer. Like the one in which a high school guy sees a girl being hassled and steps in to protect her at the risk of his life. Despite his physical weaknesses, he's able to defend her, and she sees him in a new, attractive, romantic light. That was only one of several.

I'm not saying they were *good*.

"Okay," I said to Sydney. Nice and unassuming.

"Mr. Konigsberg invited me to be on the debate team this year," Syd began. "Which puts me right in the middle of the drama department."

Mr. Konigsberg was the speech and debate team coach, while Mrs. Goldie ran the acting and technical side of things. Their classrooms were just down the hall from each other.

"Oh," I said. "Okay . . ."

"So I need to know— Well, I mean, we're not going to talk about her like last year before we got together, right?"

"No," I said, too quickly.

"You sure?"

"I guess," I said.

"Well, I'd rather we didn't," Syd said, sounding about forty-five years old and divorced twice and unflappable. "I mean, we've got *us* going on now."

"Yeah," I said.

"So you understand?"

"Sure I do."

I didn't, but I couldn't say it. She hadn't grasped that when I said "No," what I meant was, *No, I can't promise I won't talk about Rebecca or think about her or wish someday we . . .*

"Great!" Sydney said, smiling happily. She had a great smile.

Sydney sat up, straddled my leg, sat back on her heels, and peeled up her T-shirt, exposing a lacy white bra. It kind of surprised me—the style, I mean, compared to her usual buttoned-down appearance.

Oh, hell, who am I kidding, I was just surprised, period. It was the first time she'd done that. I want it noted that I did not think about Becky for the next hour or so.

Possibly a personal record.

* * * * *

"Sydney?" I say into my phone. It's been at least a minute since either of us spoke.

"What did *she* want?" Syd asks.

"I dunno, she was upset about something, I think."

"You going to go *comfort* her?"

"I'm not doing this, Syd. I'm not having this conversation, not again, not ever."

I can practically feel her scowl over the phone.

"Tell Pink Floyd we say hi!" Robby calls. Justin, on cue, begins giggling.

I give them both the finger. I love these guys, I really do. They've put up with a lot of my crap these past three years. Making fun of Syd's name—Syd Barrett, by the way, was a founding member of Pink Floyd—is a small price to ask for their patience.

"Tyler," Syd says, and sighs. "I read the story."

Despite summer creeping up on us, a chill wind blows through the park. I hunch my shoulders against it.

At least, I think it's the wind.

"Story?"

"In the magazine," Syd says. "I'm looking at it right now. Your mom gave me her copy."

Traitor. Or is it "traitoress"?

"The magazine?" I say. God help me if I'm ever on trial for something; the jury would take one look at my face and convict me on the spot.

"I'm not stupid, Ty," Syd says. "Your mom thought it was about me. But we both know that's not true, don't we?"

The wind kicks up again.

.   .   .   .   .

The first day of tenth grade, Becky walked right up to me in between my math and Spanish classes. It was the first time I'd seen her since summer vacation began. She hadn't changed much; her hair was a little shorter, like she'd gotten it cut and styled yesterday, but otherwise—

"Are you Tyler Darcy?" she said.

She'd never talked to me before. I'd never heard her *speak* before, apart from in *A Midsummer Night's Dream,* but it's not like that was her real speaking voice, you know? Her voice now tickled my spine like a breeze and made my toes curl inside my shoes. I smelled a faint aroma of vanilla on her clothes. I'd never eat vanilla ice cream the same way again.

All the scripts I'd written in my head turned out to be empty pages as soon as she spoke. A year of imagining, hoping, waiting; now she had made the first move, and I couldn't think of a single clever, charming, romantic thing to say. All I could do was answer.

"Yes?" I said, question mark and all.

"And you're going out with Sydney Barrett?"

"Yes?" I repeated, not enjoying the reminder.

Becky studied my face, holding a textbook to her chest with both arms. A black leather backpack hanging from her shoulders had replaced her blue messenger bag from last year. I wondered crazily if she had animal crackers stashed inside.

"Huh," she said.

I tried to lick my lips, but my tongue was stuck to the roof of my mouth.

"Well . . . see ya," Becky said.

"Okay," I said.

Becky walked off down the hall. I watched her until she turned a corner. Right then, for the first time, it occurred to me that she was always alone. Not once freshman year had I seen her talking to anyone in the halls. Previously I'd kept an eye out for any possible boyfriends, but now I realized there weren't any girls talking to her either. I knew she talked to Syd, but I never saw Becky talk to anyone myself.

Not unless you counted onstage while performing. Then she soared.

•   •   •   •   •

"You're not seriously going to try and lie to me," Sydney adds as I zip up my Dickies jacket against the wind.

I don't respond. I never lie to Sydney, not really. Evade. Excuse. Scoff. But not lie.

"When did you get it?" I say finally. "The magazine."

"I met Staci and Michelle for coffee at Jamaican Blue," Syd says. "By your house? And on the way home, I stopped by to say hi. And your mom told me about the story. Gabby didn't even know about it. Why didn't you tell her?"

Gabrielle is finishing up her college degree in digital journalism. Guess writing runs in the family. She still lives at home because, for one thing, it's too expensive for her to live on campus, never mind in an apartment. For another thing, about three years ago, right after she turned eighteen, Mom caught her getting high in the backyard with some friends. That was that. Mom and Dad said she was welcome to smoke whatever she wanted, wherever she wanted, on her dime and at her own place, and she could drive there in her own damn car. So Gabby left. That lasted about a month before she came back begging for another shot, which Mom and Dad gave her. I'd been just as glad when she left as when she came back; I'd known about the drugs and hated how it made her act so lazy, and how shitty it made her clothes reek. When she moved back in, she was more like the sister I'd known before. Someone who'd stop what she was doing to read anything I wrote, and give me advice on how to make it better.

As for not telling Gabby about this particular story yet, mainly it was because she loves Syd so much. Gabby, like

Robby and Justin, is not the president of the Becky Webb Fan Club. I'd asked Mom specifically not to show Gabby the story, not yet. Guess I should've said, "Don't show anyone, ever."

"Just didn't get around to it yet," I tell Syd.

"Well, you should've seen your mom's face. She's really proud of you."

"What are *you*?"

"Also proud. But, um . . . simultaneously, pretty pissed off. Maybe a dollop of jealous. Maybe more than a dollop, actually."

"Syd . . ."

"Where are you exactly? What park? I think it's time we had a chat about your mistress."

"Okay, *that* is so totally not true," I say. "Come on."

"Where, Tyler."

"Not tonight."

"Yes, tonight."

"You're overreacting," I say, knowing that really, given her tone, she's taking it all quite well, considering what she read.

"You wrote a love story about another girl," Sydney states. I hear paper rustling. " 'When she danced, my eyes swapped places, putting everything else out of focus, leaving her physical masterpiece the only light on which to rely for vision,' " Syd quotes.

I hear the magazine being flung away. "Could you get any more sappy? Plus, she's a sucky dancer."

I disagree, but have the sense to do it in silence.

. . . . .

I'd always assumed Becky had friends in the drama department, and assumed Sydney was among them. The day Becky first talked to me in the hall, watching her walk away, trying to drink in every detail of her red board shorts, her lightly tanned smooth calves, her sandals, her black T-shirt, the raised outline of the back of her bra pressed against the jersey material, the peach fuzz on the back of her neck tapering up to her same adorable haircut . . . I wondered, *How does she know about Syd and me?*

Because, it would turn out, Sydney had talked to her that morning in the drama department.

And kindly advised Becky to, quote, "stay out of my way."

. . . . .

"So you were going to go to Rebecca's house?" Syd says through my silence.

"Yes, Sydney, I was. Past tense. I'm not going there now. It's no big."

"Going to your crush's house in the middle of the night because she called you on a whim?" Sydney says. "That's a very *big*, Tyler."

It's only, like, ten o'clock, I say to myself. I know better than to say it to Syd. My buzz is wearing off very quickly.

"She's not my crush!" I say.

All right, I stand corrected: I *do* lie to Sydney when it comes to how I feel about Becky. And Sydney, assuredly, knows it.

"Why do you do this to me?" Sydney says. To her credit, any other girl probably would've been all weepy or screaming. Like the chicks Justin and Robby date. But not Syd. She still sounds twice, three times as old as she really is. She's upset, sure, but not melting down like any other reasonable seventeen-year-old girl.

"I'm not doing anything to you, Syd," I say. "She's a friend, and that's all she's ever been, and all she ever will be, and Jesus! You know all that! Gimme a break!"

"So you're not going over there?"

"No."

"But only because you've been drinking and can't drive."

"If that's what you need to tell yourself."

"I need *you* to tell me, Ty."

"Whatever. I gotta go."

"Fine."

The line goes dead. For a moment, I consider throwing my cell as hard and far as I can. But that would be stupid.

Which is to say, completely in character for me.

· · · · ·

If I didn't know I was officially in a relationship before school started sophomore year, it was made clear our first day back during lunch.

Syd and I were together in Honors English again, and she sat beside me like she had the previous year. Which was fine, because we still got into debates and arguments and discussions about the reading assignments, and had a good time doing it. We had Ms. Hochhalter again, which was awesome. But that first day, I was still reeling from Becky's sudden contact, and anxious to get to the cafeteria and see if anything else had changed about her. Or us.

Sydney grasped my hand as we walked out of English together and gave me one of her big smiles. "So, where do you want to sit during lunch?" she asked.

I almost came to a complete stop but managed to keep it to an awkward stumble. "Sit?" I said. Because I'm cool like that.

"Don't you eat in the cafeteria?" Syd asked.

"Uh . . . yeah," I said. "With Robby and Justin."

"Cool," Sydney said. "Is it okay if I come with?"

There was, of course, only one answer to that. "Sure," I said.

"Great!" Syd said. "I'll see you then."

After chemistry, I met Syd at the doors to the cafeteria. Admittedly, I did enjoy watching all the incoming freshmen look around the cafeteria like it was a slaughterhouse, eyes wide or pretend-narrowed for toughness. I was coming up on sixteen, and somehow managed to be nostalgic for fourteen.

It didn't occur to me until then that Syd and I hadn't sat together before. Maybe she didn't like Robby and Justin, maybe she already had a special place she liked to sit, or maybe she didn't want to look all committed and possessive. I don't know, and I never asked.

We got our lunches and found Robby and Justin sitting

59

at the table we'd occupied last year. Only this time, they each sat beside a girl, and not the ones I'd met—correction, seen—last year at the mall.

And Becky sat at her same table as well, on a corner. Also alone. Well, alone in the sense that no one was talking to her, anyway; she had empty seats on her left as well as across from her, but there were other people at the table. Freshmen, I thought.

But at least she was facing me.

Or would have been, had I grabbed the seat I'd intended to.

"Hey, what's up, Pink Floyd?" Robby said as Sydney took the seat I'd been aiming for.

"Nothing much," Syd said. "Who's Pink Floyd?"

Justin snorted and shook his head, taking a big bite of his hamburger.

"Nothing, nothing," Robby said. "Hey, man, are you going to sit or what?"

It took me a second to realize he was talking to me. And that I was, indeed, standing.

"Yeah," I said. And sat across from Sydney, my back to Becky. The instant my ass touched the seat, I thought, *You wanted me to sit this way, didn't you?* And for no reason—no legitimate reason—I got utterly and completely furious.

"Hey, so this is Staci," Robby announced, smiling broadly and gesturing to the girl next to him.

"Hi!" Staci said to us.

"Michelle," Justin said, waving his burger absently at the girl next to him.

Michelle, looking none too thrilled with this introduction, smacked Justin across the shoulder. Justin cowered sarcastically before laughing with his mouth full.

"Hi," Sydney said, immediately friendly. Of course. "Sydney. I don't know what the whole Pink Floyd thing is all about."

"Nobody does," Michelle said. "Robby's always got some—"

"Why don't you look it up?" I said, my jaw barely moving.

Michelle paused. "Look . . . what up?"

"Nothing. Never mind." I shoved a French fry into my mouth and chomped it to death, but I have to say, fries just don't have that anger-satisfying crunch.

"Are you okay?" Syd asked me softly.

"Oh, I'm just *ducky*." It was this thing my mom said when she was mad.

Syd stared at me for a second, then picked up her tray. "Okay. I think maybe I'll eat outside today." She stood up. "Nice to meet you," she said to the girls, and walked through the cafeteria to the exit, tray in hand.

The other four turned to look at me.

"What's your deal?" Michelle said.

Still pissed, and I mean righteously set to deck someone, I eyeballed her and said, "I'm sorry, you matter because?"

"Whoa," Justin said, but very quietly.

"Ex-*cuse* me!" Michelle said, and stood up.

"Hey, man . . . ," Justin said to me.

"What?" I said, louder than I meant to. I think. "She your girlfriend now? It's the first day of school—how'd you even meet her? Huh?"

"Dude," Justin said, frowning.

"You're an *asshead*!" Michelle declared.

"Jerk," Staci added.

I turned to face Staci. "Did we have a class last year?" I asked her.

"Maybe . . ."

"I thought so," I said. "Have you gained weight since then?"

Staci gasped and covered her mouth. She bolted up and away, with Michelle squealing after her.

Gotta say—it felt good.

Until my two friends zeroed in on me.

"Wow," Robby said calmly, folding his hands on the table, quite possibly in an effort to keep from tearing my jaw off. "That was impressive, Ty. Now do you mind, please, explaining to us what the almighty holy fuck just happened here?"

I tried not to. I really, really tried not to. But I looked over my shoulder before answering.

"I dunno," I said as the anger drained out of me. Becky sat reading a book, but I couldn't see the title. I wanted to get up and go ask her what it was.

Justin turned his head too, to see what I was looking at.

When he figured it out, he said, "Wait a sec. Are you still crushing on that chick?"

"Looks that way," I said.

I faced our table again and saw that Robby had relaxed a bit. "What about Syd?" he asked. "Did you just break up here or what?"

"I don't know," I said. I tossed another fry into my mouth. It was already cold. "Sorry about the girls."

They both shrugged. "Just met 'em," Robby admitted. Then he laughed and picked up my hamburger. He took a huge bite and put it back on my plate. I guess that made us even in his book.

"Did you gain weight," he said, shaking his head. "That was awesome."

* * * * *

I'm still debating chucking my cell when I get another text. This time from Gabby.

Congratulations on the pub! Also, you're a dick. :)

So's your face, I write back. It's an inside joke of ours. No matter how ridiculous or plain a sentence might be, we always follow it with "So's your face."

Gabby sends another text. *Why didn't you tell me?*

I text back as I walk slowly toward the table. *It's no big deal.*

LQR is a huge deal, Gabby writes. *And you really hurt Syd. Idiot.*

I stop short. Even though Robby and Justin are all of ten

feet away and arguing loudly about who the world's best lead guitar player is, I barely register them. Gabby's text glares from my screen.

I don't know what to write back. I didn't *mean* to hurt Sydney. And I'd love nothing more than to argue with my sister, come up with some plausible deniability, but Gabrielle's no liar. If she says Syd is hurt by the story, then it's true.

What did she say? I write.

Nothing, Gabby writes. *She didn't have to. Fix this, bro.*

I wander back to the table. Justin has the champagne bottle upended over his red Solo cup and is slapping the base for the last possible drops of alcohol.

"So, how'd it go with ol' Pink Floyd?" he asks, and laughs.

"Shut up."

"I don't wanna tell you your business or anything," Robby says. "But . . ."

"I know, I know, I know, okay?"

I sit on the bench beside Justin and hold my head in both hands. I've got the vague whisper of a headache starting behind my skull.

Robby socks my shoulder. Ow.

"It's not fair, man," he says. "To Pink Floyd. You can't drag her around like that."

I don't say anything.

four

· · · · ·

I didn't tell Syd about running into Becky that first day of sophomore year. I wasn't trying to deceive her or anything; I mean, it wasn't like I'd hooked up with Becky. Syd had asked me not to talk about Becky anymore, so I didn't.

Not even when Sydney cornered me after school.

"Okay?" she asked, falling into step beside me as I trudged toward the bus stop. "You calmed down now?"

"Yeah," I said. I didn't think I was lying about that.

"Want to tell me what the hell happened?"

No answer would be sufficient. I sure couldn't tell her the truth, and I wasn't a good enough liar to come up with anything convincing.

"Bad day," I said. Which I suppose was the truth.

"Well, you hit Staci pretty hard," Sydney said as we turned left toward the parking lot. "She's had eating issues."

Okay, that honestly did make me feel bad. I'd pulled the "gained weight" comment out of thin air; I hadn't recognized Staci at all.

"I'm sorry," I said.

"Don't tell me, tell her," Syd said. "You can tell her this weekend when me and her and Michelle go out for coffee."

"You're going—what?"

Sydney nodded. "I caught them on the way out of the cafeteria, trying to get away from *you*, in fact, and we had lunch together. And made plans."

Perfect.

We'd reached the parking lot. I'd need to cut left and follow the sidewalk to the east side of the school for my bus. Sydney always got a ride from her dad, but they lived in the complete opposite direction from me.

Sydney and I stopped together on the sidewalk. Over her shoulder, I saw Becky Webb coming out of the drama department and heading for the parking lot. She stopped and sat down on the curb, in her usual spot. I'd watched her all last year sitting or standing there, always getting picked up by that flashy SUV.

"So will you?" Syd asked.

I couldn't take my eyes off Becky. Was it just me, or was she specifically avoiding looking in our direction? Like she knew we were standing there and didn't want me to know she knew it? Probably not . . . but maybe . . .

"Tyler?"

"Hmm? What? Yeah. Okay. Wait, do what, now?"

Sydney shook her head, leaned up, and kissed me once on the lips. "You're hopeless," she said. "I'd appreciate it if you'd man up and apologize to Staci and Michelle on Friday night. I wouldn't turn one down, myself, but, you know. Whatever."

"I'm sorry," I said right away. "Really."

"Thank you."

At that moment, a red sports car squealed into the lot and rocketed between rows of parked cars. The driver damn near executed a one-eighty skid to pull up to where Becky was waiting. Syd and I both watched as Becky brought her hands to her hair, as if frustrated, and got into the car. Before the door had even closed, the driver took off, spraying loose rocks onto the sidewalk and earning no less than three middle fingers from various students in and around the lot.

"Wow, asshole," Syd commented as the car disappeared down the same street the SUV used to take last year.

"Right," I agreed. I wanted desperately to know who the driver was. Her mom? Dad?

Boyfriend?

Syd turned back to me. "So just give me a call Friday night. I'll let you know where we end up."

"How am I supposed to get to wherever you are?"

"Just tell Gabrielle," Sydney said. "She loves me."

Couldn't argue that point. And Syd knew about Gabby's deal with my parents: she got a car but also had to agree to be my taxi on the weekends.

"There's my dad," Sydney said. "You sure there's nothing you want to talk about? About today at lunch? Or anything that happened before lunch?"

That's when I knew. I saw it in her face. She knew I'd talked to Becky that morning. Or at least suspected.

"Nope," I said. "I'm good."

Her dad pulled up to the sidewalk. "Okay," Syd said, kissing me again. "See you tomorrow."

I waved to her dad, who gave me a little salute thing back. Once Syd was in the car, I turned and headed for my bus.

"Hey, muchacho," Robby greeted me as I sat beside him. "It's the first day back, and already this bus thing is getting old. We need a car."

"Uh-huh," I said, staring out the window.

"Right," Robby said, and put on his headphones. "Say no more, brother."

One great thing about Robby: the guy took a great hint.

The next day, I passed Becky in the hall again. Turned out we'd be repeating this encounter every day because of where our respective second-hour classes were located. She'd be on her way to math; I'd be on my way to chemistry.

I wanted to say something. Again, "hi" might've been a good start. But I didn't. And neither did she.

But we made eye contact. Oh yes, we saw each other.

Sometimes she gave me a nod and a smile—small, barely registering. Other times a smirk, which to me read like, *Why on God's green earth are you going out with Sydney Barrett, you great feeb?*

Maybe I was projecting my own thoughts onto her expression. I don't know.

I continued hanging out and hooking up with Sydney. We'd eat lunch together, sometimes with Robby and Justin and some other people from Justin's art class. With Michelle and Staci off their radar because "they were too clingy," the guys moved on to other potential ex-girlfriends. Justin flirted endlessly and hopelessly with this tall granola-soy junior named Holly who made "sublime ecoterrorist sculptures" out of plastic utensils. He had no chance, and he knew it, but I gave the guy credit: he kept trying, which was more than I could say about myself. Robby brought a new girl to the table every few weeks or so, but he didn't seem to really fall for any of them. Mostly he kept the whole table laughing, as usual.

Becky ate alone. Reading a book, or staring out the windows. There was nothing to see, just a row of classrooms about ten yards or so from the cafeteria. I always wondered what she was thinking about.

Every school has freaky kids, right? The easy targets. Because she was always by herself, I started expecting someone to rag on her, maybe throw something at her, laugh at her.

Part of me wanted it to happen, to be honest, so I'd have

a reason to stand up and deliver this full-throated baritone monologue about leaving her alone or facing my wrath. Maybe, if I was lucky, it would be followed by a slow clap from the rest of the students in the cafeteria.

That was another version of the story I was writing about her.

But no one ever gave her any grief that I saw. She left people alone, and they left her alone.

I felt like we were dancing. Not together, not at a dimly lit gym prom or anything. But—*maneuvering*. Jockeying for position. The daily, silent half smiles and nods in the hall meant something, didn't they? They had to. Or maybe I needed them to.

At lunch one day about a month into sophomore year, the cover of the book Becky was reading had an excellent illustration of a dragon on the cover. A fantasy novel. And that got me thinking.

STALEMATE
by Tyler Darcy

The elf wore only an iridescent sash spun from spider silk. She perched high in a pine tree, clinging to a decaying branch with talon toes. The elf stood, balanced precariously on the tired old limb. She inhaled deeply—and relaxed her grip.

She fell, gravity yanking her feet. Then, like whips, her limber fingers lashed out and caught the branch. She arched her delicate, feline spine once, twice, then flew through the night sky.

A pinprick of light in the distance beckoned her, and she veered unerringly toward it. The light was a campfire, burning brightly and with no remorse. In its warmth dozed a knight, his armor patiently reflecting the surroundings nearby.

The elf landed without sound, laughing to herself; *she* had no reflection.

The knight awoke with a start, his hand falling to his sword hilt. The elf met his eyes, and locked with them in mortal, silent combat.

He spoke her name, his voice trembling. The elf laughed tinkling bells but did not answer. She paced toward him, like mercury over iron, passing through brambles that earlier had sliced the warrior's clothing.

"Dance with me," she purred, and pulled a crimson scarf from some unseen place in her sash. The elf snapped it toward him and giggled.

The knight leaped to his feet and slashed at her shapely form, his face twisted with rage. She contorted her body slightly, letting the blade slip past her milky belly. Giggling again, she pirouetted, waving the scarf and coiling it around the blade in a lover's embrace. She tugged lightly on the scarf, sending the weapon soaring into the darkness.

The knight retreated, pulling a dagger from

his boot. On and on the girl laughed. The warrior swung the dagger with a rage resembling glee, but the elf moved like the flame of a candle, insubstantial and beautiful. She whipped the scarf at him, one corner cutting deeply across his cheek. The knight licked blood from his face and roared.

Through the night they danced together. The knight's clothing became a bloody latticework, while the elf skipped and pranced without injury.

As dawn arrived gray and cold, the knight threw aside his weapon and leaped at the elf. He gripped her wrists, clamping them against her thighs. The knight leaned forward and smashed a kiss against her apple lips, then withdrew.

The girl laughed again as she had at the beginning. She waved the scarf at him one final time and was gone, leaving the scarlet cloth to float gently to the ground.

· · · • •

"You remember that sort of fantasy story I wrote sophomore year?" I ask Robby. "The real short one for English?"

He belches. "Um . . . no. And don't change the subject. I'm talking about Sydney."

"So am I, actually."

"I 'member it," Justin says. He spies into the bottle, which must be bone-dry by now, and makes as if to throw it into the parking lot. I tense, waiting for him to send the bottle hurtling to the concrete and smashing to bits, but then he laughs and sets the bottle down on the table.

"The chick was hot," Justin says.

"How do you know?" I ask. "I didn't describe her."

"That was the thing," Justin says. "You didn't have to. The dude wanted her. That's all you had to say."

Sometimes, Justin is a right royal idiot. Other times, he nails it.

"Interesting," I say, frowning at my sneakers.

"But that 'milky belly' thing, that was hysterical!" Justin adds, cackling. "Miiiiilky beeeelly!"

He's really cracking himself up now.

"What can I say?" I tell him, and sigh dramatically. "I was young."

That gets them both going. Excellent. Once they've calmed back down, though, Justin adds, "It was about, like—*desire*. They were acting like they wanted to kill each other, but really they were totally flirting."

"You remember all that?" I can't help but be a little flattered.

"Yeah, man," Justin says. "It was sexy."

"What did Sydney think of it?" Robby says, narrowing his eyes at me. I can't tell if he's still drunk or not. Or, come to think of it, if he really was to begin with. Justin did the most damage to the champagne.

"I don't think she ever . . ."

I stop as Robby raises his hands. "You never let her read it, did ya."

". . . No."

"Which is why you gotta figure yourself out," Robby says. "Man, that's your *girl*. Shit or get off the pot, know what I mean?"

I nod slowly. And think about Gabby's last text: *Fix this*.

* * * * *

Right after I wrote "Stalemate," I started considering getting into the drama department.

I couldn't very well drop any of my classes and take Drama Two—you had to take Drama One first anyway, and I didn't want to get onstage—but our speech, debate, and theater club, Masque & Gavel, met after school. Robby called it "Massengill." Sydney always attended the meetings, because she was on the debate team.

Since I couldn't ask Syd about Becky anymore, I figured joining the club would be a good way to see how Becky got along with the drama club weirdos. Yes, I dubbed Sydney a drama weirdo, too. She knew it and never argued the point.

"So, what do you guys do in the drama club, anyway?" I asked Sydney a few days after it occurred to me to join Masque & Gavel.

"Eh, talk about the plays and speech competitions, mostly," Sydney said.

We were sitting near the parking lot after school, waiting for my mom to come pick us up. It was a Friday, which meant Syd was coming over for dinner, a movie, and making out until her dad came to get her. Not having a car sucked. And as far as getting together was concerned, we were limited in what we dared with my bedroom door open; i.e., not much.

I didn't see Becky waiting for her ride. Hadn't lately, in fact.

"Usually there's either rehearsal for a play or practice for a tournament afterward," she added. "Why? You thinking of joining?"

I shrugged. "Nah," I said. Fairly convincingly, I thought. "I'm not an actor."

"You don't have to be an actor," Syd said. "You could learn how to run lights or sound. Or help build the sets. Or why don't you write a play? Maybe they'd let you put it on."

That actually caught my ear, for real. For a minute there, I actually forgot about Becky.

No, that's a lie. Moved her temporarily to a different location in my brain, maybe.

"You think so?"

"I couldn't promise you, but it's worth asking," Syd said. "Have you ever written a play?"

"Nope. Just stories." My short piece about Becky was on its one hundredth draft by that point. Not the fantasy story—the heroic, romantic one I'd been revising every month since I'd first written it the year before.

"But *good* stories," Sydney said, kissing my cheek.

Maybe that was another reason I stayed with Syd. She liked my writing. I didn't really do anything with it except give a few of what I thought were the funnier ones to her, Robby, and Justin to read. But I figured I could write a play. It would be just like a story, only without the description. God knows I had enough experience dreaming up dialogue for Becky to follow with me as leading man. Even if I never wrote it down.

"Thanks," I said, and I meant it. "Maybe I will."

"There's a meeting on Monday," Sydney said. "You could come with me if you wanted. Just to meet . . . people . . ."

Syd paused and scrutinized me. "This isn't about Rebecca Webb, is it, Ty?"

"What? No."

"Are you sure?"

"Syd. Come on."

"You spent half of last year going on about her. And I'm not stupid."

"I didn't say you were stupid!"

"Then tell me. Tell me this newfound interest in Masque and Gavel has nothing to do with her."

My mom pulled up and waved at us through the window. She, like my sister, loved Syd. Which didn't make it any easier to consider breaking up with her.

I stood up. "I'm not even going to dignify that with a response," I said, half joking, half scared to death that I was as transparent as Mom's windshield.

Sydney stood up too. "All right," she said. "Forget I said anything. Think about it this weekend, maybe write some ideas down."

"Cool," I said, and opened the passenger door for her.

I did think about it all weekend. Even wrote a few pages of five or six different play ideas.

All of them ended up centering around a guy who likes this girl. . . .

I didn't print out any of these ideas. And didn't finish even a whole scene.

Yet Monday after school, I went to my first drama club meeting.

Becky Webb sat in the front row, farthest corner to my right. Like in the cafeteria, there was an empty chair to her side and behind her. As if she was shielded from the rest of the class. I saw a couple people give her nods as they stomped through the rows to find seats, and she'd look up and smile toothlessly. Most of these greeters were guys.

So she did have friends here. But then why did she still look so isolated?

. . . . .

"I don't even know why she likes me," I say.

"Who? You mean Sydney or Becky?" Justin asks, rubbing his belly like it's about to revolt again.

"Syd. I already know Becky doesn't like me. Not like that, anyway."

"You don't know why Syd digs you?" Robby says. "I'll tell you why. It's because you're swinging a poleax down there!"

I stare at him. "Dude . . . *what?*"

77

"Hell yeah," Robby goes. "I can tell just by looking at ya. There's no cork in that bat. That's a hundred percent American grade A steel, dude."

"... *What?*"

"I think he's saying you have a big dick," Justin reports, and burps. He sighs happily afterward and sinks down on the bench. Belly crisis averted.

"Yeah, I got the tweet, but why's he saying it?"

Justin shrugs. Robby laughs and punches my shoulder again. Ow. Again.

"I'm messing with you, Ty," he says. "Damn, I thought the booze would relax you."

"Yeah," I say. "Me too." I am about as close to sober as a guy can get despite the alcohol. Maybe Western Flower is a cheap champagne.

"How do you know she doesn't like you?" Justin asks. "Becky, I mean. Why'd she call you tonight if she didn't have a thing for you?"

"We're friends," I remind him. This isn't news.

Justin pulls on an extraordinarily doubtful look. Robby gets up and stands in front of me. "I don't think friends do the kinda things she's done," he says. "I mean, talk about blue balls."

I try to glare up at him. *He* knows that *I* know exactly what he's referring to.

Robby ignores my glare and holds out his arms.

"Just sayin'," he goes. "It wasn't cool of her."

Justin, on the other hand, I didn't tell about the shower incident at Becky's house. "Hold up," Justin says. "What'd she do?"

"You wanna tell him, or you want me to?" Robby asks.

I wish my phone would ring again. Even if it's Sydney.

•　•　•　•　•

Sydney and I didn't sit near Becky at the drama club meeting. We sat in the middle, surrounded by Syd's drama friends. And when I say "drama friends," I mean they were about the most dramatic bunch of people I'd ever heard speak. You would've thought they were discussing which of them was going to win an Academy Award, the way they went on about casting for the next play, *To Kill a Mockingbird*.

"You are auditioning, right, Sydney?" some girl demanded. "Oh my god. You must. Positively. Oh my god!"

"Oh my god" was right. Their voices hurt my ears. I tried not to get caught watching Becky, who was sitting quietly in that corner chair, her backpack on her lap.

"I don't know," Sydney said. "Probably not, but it depends on how debate goes."

Another girl, with hair dyed three different colors like a neon Neapolitan ice-cream cone, said, "What about your boyfriend?" and poked my ribs. "He should! He's hot!"

It was the first time anyone had used those two words to describe me. You can figure out which two.

"Ah, no, no thanks," I said, waving the Neapolitan girl off.

"We totally don't have enough boys," she pressed on. "Just, like, Matthew and them. You *have* to!"

Syd grinned at me. I forced myself not to glance in Becky's direction.

"Well . . . we'll see," I said, hoping that would make them shut up.

"I will if you will," Sydney said.

"Maybe I should start with lights or sound, like you said," I reminded her.

We didn't get to talk any more about it right then because the club officers—all juniors and seniors—ran into the room, whooping and screaming and waving their arms around.

I almost left right then. It was way too much energy for me. Robby and Justin were plenty.

Because the meeting was pretty much about boring stuff like the upcoming auditions and where the next speech tournament was, I clandestinely observed Becky. She barely moved a muscle. Just sat there, listening intently. At least she had taken a notebook out of her bag and took notes during all the announcements.

"Now, you guys, seriously," the president of the club said, waving his arms in the air. What was it with drama kids and waving their arms? "We really need some fresh new techie blood for this show. Nick's moving to New York . . ."

Everyone shouted "Boooo!" A stringy dude wearing a vest and bowler hat stood up, bowed, and sat back down.

". . . which totally sucks," the president said. "So we're gonna need some people in the booth for this show. Ask your friends—"

"Tyler will do it!" Sydney shouted.

Fifty heads spun toward me. Mine spun toward Sydney. Syd sat on my right, and beyond her was Becky. Who also looked at me as if noticing for the first time that I was there.

Our eyes met. I wasn't sure, but I think she smiled.

"Um," I said.

"Is this your first meeting, Tyler?" the president asked.

"Uh . . . yeah."

"*VIRGIN ALERT!*" everyone screamed in unison. And they all pounded their feet on the floor and clapped while the officers took a lap around their chairs at the front of the room. Waving their arms, of course.

Believe it or not, for one heartbeat of time, I didn't realize "virgin" meant it was my first *drama club meeting*. Me, insecure? Never.

While I tried to disappear into my seat, I noticed Becky smiling for real, clapping her hands with everyone else. Like she was really enjoying my embarrassment.

Sydney was too busy egging everyone on to notice me smile back at Becky.

Between Sydney and the whole damn club making such a big racket and the look on Becky's face as she watched me, I pretty much had to say yes.

•   •   •   •   •

I gear up to tell Robby what he can do with my big dick, when my cell buzzes again.

"What did Becky do?" Justin demands from both of us. "C'mon, man!"

I check my phone. Sydney. Saved by the bell.

She's texted me: *Which park?*

I write: *Why?*

If you can't drive home I'll make sure you get there. All 3 of you. Which park?

We're fine.

"Is that Syd?" Robby asks me as I type.

"Hey, Pink Floyd!" Justin croons, and falls off the picnic table bench laughing. " '*I'll see you on the dark side of the moooooooon!*' "

I'm jealous of his condition. At least *he's* having a good time. I should be too. It's why we came here.

It's too risky, Sydney writes. *I won't be able to sleep if I*

My phone rings while I'm in the middle of reading her text.

Becky.

don't know you got home in 1 piece so which park?

I hit the green button and put the phone up to my ear.

"Becky?"

"Hey," she says. Her voice is heavy and soft, her nose vaguely plugged.

I don't want to talk to her with the guys looming, so I head toward the parking lot.

"Excuse me, sir?" Robby calls.

Right. I throw my car keys at him and walk quickly toward the parking lot. Robby, clearly understanding I want to be alone and that I'm not going to try to drive off, lets me go. God bless 'im.

"You don't sound so good, Mustardseed," I say, once I'm far enough away that they can't overhear me. "What's going on?"

"Oh, the *usual*," Becky says. Spite draws out the last word and hones it to a sharp point. "I'm reconsidering your offer to come by in a couple hours. What're you up to tonight, exactly? I didn't figure you for a drinking man."

"Just hanging at the park with Robby and Justin. Celebrating, I guess."

"Yeah? Celebrating what?"

"It's nothing, just this magazine thing."

"What magazine thing?"

I take a deep breath. I have to tread carefully here.

"I got this thing published in a magazine," I say.

"Really? That's great, Tyler. That's awesome. Congrats, man."

I hate it—*hate it*—when she calls me "man" like that. Something about the word or her delivery seems to cement my place in her world. That of Good Buddy. BFF. Like she's just another guy.

Still. She's happy for me. As happy as Becky is capable of being, anyway.

five

· · · · ·

After being bullied into it by her drama friends, Sydney ended up auditioning for *Mockingbird*, but she didn't get the part she wanted. She got no part at all, in fact.

"I'm sorry," I told her at lunch the day the cast was announced.

"Thanks, but it's not a big deal. I've got a tournament on opening night anyway."

"You'll probably take State," I said.

"Yeah?" Syd asked, eyeing me curiously, as if my encouraging her was a bad thing. "Why's that?"

"You're smart," I said. "And you don't get nervous in front of people. You think fast. It's a great fit."

Sydney smiled and gave me a kiss.

Secretly I was relieved about Syd not being in the play. Because Becky *did* get cast. Scout Finch. Pretty much the female lead.

Which, honestly, I didn't understand. Even after her bouncy performance last year in *Midsummer*, I was having trouble reconciling the quiet girl who ate lunch by herself with the energetic performer I'd seen onstage. In my stories, my Becky character typically became a world-renowned actress. And now at least—at *last*—since I was on the tech crew for the show, I'd get a chance to watch her more closely, see how she was around other people. Maybe make sure she wasn't actually dating someone from the drama department.

The first day of rehearsal scared me to death. I'd been elected to run the light board, and everyone involved in the show, from the director, Mrs. Goldie, to the makeup crew kids and technicians—or "techies"—like me had to be there for the first read-through.

I'd be in an after-school activity with Becky Webb. Exposed to a side of her I'd never gotten to see before. And vice versa. I just hoped I didn't say or do something galactically stupid when she was around.

Turned out I didn't have to say much of anything besides my name at the first rehearsal. We met in Mrs. Goldie's classroom, where she'd moved all the desks into a big circle. She made everyone say their name and role or backstage position. So I said, "Tyler Darcy, lights," and that was it.

Someone had to nudge Becky when it was her turn. She was studying her script so seriously she was biting her lower lip. Gotta say—it was kind of sexy.

"What? Oh. Becky Webb, I'm playing Scout."

"Everyone knows Becca," some girl said, not quietly, and nearly everyone laughed. Becky didn't. She just went back to her script.

That maybe should've been a clue. But let's see: Male? Check. Teenager? Check. In love? Check. Yep, those clues were destined to rocket straight over my head.

It was the first time I discovered she called herself Becky rather than Rebecca. I didn't understand why someone would then call her Becca, but didn't quite want to ask in public. *So that's what she goes by,* I thought. A new facet to ponder. *Becky. Becky.* It felt like a spotlight had been shined on her, revealing something new and wonderful.

It sort of made up for the fact that she hadn't seemed to notice that I was there. I mean, we'd seen each other at the meeting . . . in the hallway every day . . . but at that first rehearsal, she just kept her face buried in her script.

I'd read *To Kill a Mockingbird* before, for an English class, and the play stuck to the book's story pretty closely. I guess I liked it. I mean, it was a great book and all. But mostly I kept my script up in front of my face just high enough to somewhat conceal my spying on Becky. The Neapolitan chick and a couple of other girls Syd had talked to at the Massengill meeting seemed to keep an eye on *me,* but when I looked at them, they just looked away. I got dizzy trying to balance my spying on Becky with not getting caught doing it by Syd's friends.

I spent the next two weeks after school getting a crash course on the lighting system in our auditorium from the stringy guy, Nick. He was cool, though. Pretty laid-back. I had trouble concentrating sometimes, because from the booth—the upstairs room at the back of the auditorium, where I'd control all the lights—I had a clear view all the way down to the stage, where Becky was more often than not.

It wasn't until after Nick moved away that I spoke to Becky for the second time in my life.

I was on a ladder onstage, struggling with a wrench to attach a lighting instrument to a black steel pipe, when I heard her voice.

"Hey."

I damn near fell off the ladder. Becky slid slowly across the stage, which was bare except for some colored tape on the floor showing where the set was going to be built.

We were alone.

"Hey," I said back, trying to sound casual. Like *hell* I wasn't an actor!

"So you're the new Nick," she said, letting her black backpack slip off her shoulder to the ground. She sat down right in the middle of the stage next to it, watching me.

I cleared my throat. "Um, yeah. I guess so. I don't have a cool hat, though. Or a vest."

She nodded in mock seriousness. "I think they issue them on opening night."

I laughed, probably too loud, and Becky smiled. She looked tired, as if the impression she gave of serenity was actually just exhaustion.

I climbed down from the ladder and forced myself to walk over to her. I could hear my heartbeat in my ears, feel it thump in my toes. I wondered if Sydney could hear it all the way in the debate room, where she was at that moment preparing a case or an argument or whatever against the death penalty.

"So, I guess technically we haven't really met," I said to Becky, stopping about five feet away. "I'm Tyler Darcy."

"Mistah Dahcie," Becky said with a British accent.

I nodded helplessly. A lot of girls have seen and adore all those *Pride and Prejudice* movies, with various hot guys playing Mr. Fitzwilliam Darcy. And of course in the movies they all have these silly accents.

Although when Becky said it, it felt a little different.

"I'm Becky," she added.

"Becky. Hi."

"Hi."

"So, wait, is it Becca or Becky?" I asked, because I'd continued to hear other drama students refer to her as Becca.

"Becky," she said. I thought, at the time, I saw anger flash in her eyes when she said it. I didn't dare ask why.

"Becky. Got it. Cool." I cleared my throat again. "I saw you in *Midsummer* last year," I added. "You were great."

Becky covered her mouth, as if she wasn't allowed to smile. "Thanks," she said. "It was fun."

"This is a big part," I went on, trying not to let myself babble. "Scout, I mean."

She shrugged but kept the shy little smile on. "I guess."

At which point I hit a complete and total brick wall. I had absolutely nothing else to say. Nothing that wouldn't have sent her screaming from the auditorium, anyway. I tried leafing through all the make-believe scripts I'd been working on since that first day of freshman year in the cafeteria, before remembering they'd self-deleted from my head when Becky first talked to me in the hall a month or so ago. I had nothing to fall back on.

"So, you're still dating Syd," Becky said.

I knew this made me a dick, but I could feel my face fall as I said, "Yeah . . . I guess."

Becky turned her head a bit, so her chin rested near her shoulder. Her eyelids were at half-mast. "You guess, huh?"

Was it that this gesture was *universally* sexy, or that *any* move she made was sexy to me? Couldn't tell ya.

". . . I guess," I said.

And she laughed.

I'd never heard her laugh before. Okay, I'd barely heard her *speak* before, at least "out of character." Invisible fingers tickled up my vertebrae and pulled me straight up, shoulders back, head afloat.

"Well, your secret's safe with me," Becky said.

"She's really nice," I said, knowing I sounded like a total dork. I would add that to my list right under "splendid abdominals."

"Most people are, when you finally see them," Becky replied.

It took a second for me to pick up on the fact that she was quoting from the play. Before I could form a response, she dug into her bag, pulled out her script, flipped it open, and started reading.

I didn't know if that meant we were done or what. It didn't matter, though, because I heard the backstage doors opening and voices spilling in from the back hallway. I suddenly didn't want to be caught talking to her, like we were doing something wrong. Which we weren't, of course. But I couldn't shake the feeling.

"Got any pot, Mistah Dahcie?" Becky asked, without looking up from her script.

I remember reacting physically to the question. Like I'd been jolted by the current from one of the lighting instruments. Which, it would turn out, was an omen of things to come.

"Uh . . . no," I said.

"Eh," Becky said. "Bummer. See you around?"

"Y-yeah," I stuttered. "I—I'll be around."

The rest of the cast slowly filtered into the stage space. I expected all of them to stop and stare at us, but no one did. No one except maybe Neapolitan. I still didn't know her real name. She darted quick glances at Becky, then me, before waving. At me.

"See ya," I said to Becky, semi-waving back at the neon ice-cream cone.

Becky said nothing, her forehead wrinkled in concentration.

I walked quickly through the auditorium seats to the booth, forgetting to finish plugging in the lighting instrument I'd been working on.

Got any pot? What the hell was up with that?

I watched the rehearsal from the relative privacy of the booth, struggling with Becky's question. I was not then and am not now exactly stupid when it comes to, shall we say, illicit substances. But Becky wasn't supposed to use them. Or even know about them. My Becky, my story Becky, was above that kind of thing. There wasn't room in my head for this revelation.

So by the time rehearsal had ended for the day, I'd managed to force it out of my head. *Maybe,* I told myself, *she was testing me. Maybe she doesn't want to date anyone who gets high.*

That had to be it.

· · · · ·

"What about you?" I ask Becky, kicking at the base of a light pole. "What's going on? You said you still want me to come over?"

Try not to sound *too* desperate there, cowboy.

Becky sighs softly. "It would . . . no, I don't know."

"I can," I say, because by this point, I'm positive I'm okay to drive. Getting my keys back from Robby, though, even if he *is* a bit woozy, will be a challenge. And I haven't replied to Syd's text.

"I . . . I *can't*," Becky says.

Her voice catches on the last word, like she's about to lose it. The thought of her actually crying doesn't feel quite as sexy as I'd dreamed. It just hurts.

"What is it, Becky?" I say. "What's wrong, what happened?"

"I don't know how much more I can take, Ty," she says. And though she's not crying, she's definitely holding it back.

"How much more what?"

I almost add "sweetheart," but bite it back just in time. Then I get scared, thinking her "more" is us.

"My fucking asshole parents."

Half of me gets righteously pissed then, ready to drive there right now and swing a tire iron at the Webbs' kneecaps for making her feel this way. The other half of me—I'm ashamed to say—is just relieved it's not me she's upset at.

· · · · ·

Play rehearsals lasted eight weeks. I found reasons to be at every rehearsal, even though I wasn't required to be. I still had a lot to learn about the job, I explained to Sydney. I had to meet with the stage manager, Robin. I had to meet with Mrs. Goldie about the lighting design. I had to match the *color temperatures* of the *lighting instrument filters* to the paint color of the *set*, do a *light hang* and *focus*, go through a *paper tech* with Robin . . .

I said all these things to Sydney, throwing around as

many of the theatrical terms I'd picked up as possible to make it all sound legit. Some of it was. Most wasn't.

And I was pretty sure she knew it.

"I don't remember Nick doing all that when he was running lights," Sydney said in week six.

"I couldn't say if he did or not, but he also knew his business, and I don't," I said.

"Uh-huh," Sydney said. Shaking her head, she leaned over and kissed me. "You go do whatever it is you have to do, Tyler. I'll be here."

We left it at that.

As for Becky, we'd say hi to each other every day at rehearsal. Sometimes, during a break, we'd hang out together in the auditorium seats and talk about the show. She really was good up there, no exaggeration. Maybe it was that the rest of the cast was unremarkable, but whatever. I thought she was brilliant, and I told her so.

"You're just saying that," she said one afternoon.

"No, I'm not," I said. "You really are incredible."

Becky reached over and messed up my hair. It was the first time we'd made physical contact, and it sent lightning through my body.

"Thanks. You're sweet," she said.

It wasn't "I love you, let's get together," but it came pretty close.

Speaking of lightning: a week later, I got electrocuted.

I was testing some lights behind the set to make sure all the lamps worked. This junior kid, Pete, was up in the booth, manning the light board for me. I'd plug in an instrument and yell, "Amp thirteen!" or whatever channel the light was plugged into, and Pete would power up that channel to see if the light came on or not.

This worked for the first three lights. On the fourth, Pete amped the channel just as I was plugging the instrument in, and a blue-white spark shot from the plug and burrowed into my hand. The voltage scurried up my arm, down my spine, and back up again to my skull. The next thing I knew, I was on my back looking up at the high ceiling, with Pete standing over me, laughing.

"You okay, Sparky?" he asked.

I said, "Pity . . . prissed . . . pretty . . . ," and couldn't say much else as my eyeballs traded places in my skull.

Pete laughed again and hoisted me to my feet. "Happens sometimes," he said. "Sorry, man."

I nodded weakly, and Pete hauled me to Mrs. Goldie's office, where I discovered my hair was sticking out about an inch farther from my skull than usual. I crashed on the couch in the office. Ten or fifteen minutes later, I decided all my muscles were responding appropriately to my commands. I went back to work and got a round of applause from the tech crew and calls of "Hey, Sparky!"

I waved back at them, embarrassed, and checked to see if Becky was paying attention. She was. Grinning, she wriggled her fingers at me from across the stage, and I saw her mouth make the sound *"Bzzzt!"*

That kind of made it worthwhile.

Then opening night arrived. The cast ran around all crazy and nervous. I had butterflies myself, worried I'd somehow manage to screw up pushing the big *go* button on the light board at the correct time, or that the whole damn system would crash right as we started and leave us all in the dark and it would be my fault. The guy in the booth running sound, Ross, promised it wouldn't happen.

Even Becky showed signs of stage fright. She was freaking adorable dressed as Scout Finch in overalls and a brown newsboy cap.

"Good luck," I said to her as we passed each other in the hallway behind the backstage area.

A dozen people froze and glared at me. Becky took my hand—oh dear god, thank you—and pulled me close.

"*Bad* luck," she said in a low voice. "Always say 'Break a leg' or something. Never say 'Good luck.' Okay?"

"Oh," I said. "Sorry, I didn't know." I could barely get the words out; every nerve ending in my body had migrated to my palm.

"Now you do, Sparky," she said. I still thought my new nickname was dumb, a constant reminder of my ineptitude.

But coming from her, it was great.

And then, as if her holding my hand wasn't enough, Becky stood on her tiptoes and kissed my forehead. "*That's* for luck," she whispered. "Break a leg."

"Likewise," I managed to spit out.

I didn't have to try very hard to invest her gesture with more than she probably meant. I mean, it was a *kiss*. No matter how you looked at it, Becky Webb had kissed me. Right?

This new wrinkle in our relationship—our friendship, to be more precise—panicked me as I made my way to the booth before the play began. I could barely see the light board in front of me through my delirium.

Happily, the show went off without a hitch, unless you counted Boo Radley missing his first entrance by about ten seconds because he'd fallen asleep in the dressing room. Other than that, it was great. And when Becky came out for the curtain call with the tall kid playing Atticus, the entire house—that is, all the people in the auditorium, which was full to capacity because we only had three performances total—stood and applauded. A standing ovation.

I sat in the dimly lit booth with Ross, beneath a red glare cast by the colored film we'd put over the lights, leaning back in my chair, grinning. I was so proud of her. And a small spot on my forehead still tingled from her lips.

After the curtain closed, I waited anxiously for all the audience members to file out of the auditorium. But I had to wait until they were gone before Ross and I could shut everything down and lock up the booth.

I rushed through the house and made my way backstage, which emptied into the drama department hallway. People were all over the place; the cast included more than twenty students, and everyone's family and friends were crammed into the hallway, holding flowers, talking, hugging, congratulating. I didn't see Mom, Dad, or Gabby anywhere yet, but I knew they'd make their way back.

Eagerly, I scanned the hallway for Becky, and spotted her newsboy hat a few yards away. I figured this was a great time to scam a hug from her. I mean, *everyone* was hugging everyone back there, so why not?

I almost called her name, but then figured she wouldn't be able to hear me over all the noise. I started shoving past people to get to her.

Becky was making her way to a guy wearing a dark suit and a woman in a black strapless dress. I assumed they were her parents. They wore the clothes well, unlike my dad when he had to dress up for work or business meetings; Dad was a blue-collar guy, and you could just tell his suit wasn't the best, and that he didn't know how to move in it. This guy looked like he woke up wearing an Armani. I recognized the woman as the one who'd gotten out of the SUV last year to coax Becky to get in.

From where I stood, I had sort of a profile view of the couple and of Becky as she moved toward them. I tried to get to her before she got to them. Her father's hair was jet-black, touched with distinguished gray on the sides. Her mother's blond hair was wound around the back of her head tightly, reflecting gold beneath the fluorescent lights. Becky and her mom looked a lot alike.

Wow, I thought. *Becky's got her looks.*

Becky got to them before I could reach her. *Damn it, I*

thought. I didn't want to interrupt them, at least not right away.

I was surprised to notice right then that for the money that seemed to ooze from their tanned skin, neither of her parents held flowers. You'd think they could spring for a rose or two. God knows I would have if I'd thought I could get away with it without raising Sydney's ire. Maybe they didn't know it was a tradition to give actors flowers. I hadn't known until Becky told me during one of our rehearsal breaks, just like I hadn't known to not say "Good luck."

"Dad!" Becky said. She was smiling hopefully up at him. She lost about six years wearing her costume, still looking like nine-year-old Scout approaching civic-minded Atticus.

"Hey!" her dad said. "Where's the kid who played Atticus? Have you seen his parents?"

Becky's smile dropped a little. "Atticus?" she repeated. "Oh. Um . . . Matthew Quince?"

Her dad opened the cheap photocopied playbills we'd made earlier in the week. "Right, Matthew," he said, and scanned the crowd. "Is he back here somewhere?"

"Um . . . yeah . . . ," Becky said. Her smile was gone now.

"There he is," Mr. Webb said. "And there's Don and Lydia. Let's go."

I tried to figure out who the hell Don and Lydia were as Mrs. Webb patted her hair and tossed a smile across her painted lips. Mr. Webb bustled through the crowd with his wife gliding beside him.

They came up behind Matthew, who was hugging a guy so tall he had to be Matthew's dad. Mr. Webb put a hand on Matthew's shoulder.

"Hey, here's the star!" Mr. Webb gushed. "You were just incredible, Matthew. Didn't you think so, Carla?"

"Oh, he was," Becky's mom said, putting a manicured hand on her throat. "Just wonderful!"

I turned to look at Becky. Her chin dipped, inch by inch, until she was staring at her shoes.

"Don, good to see you!" Mr. Webb said, pumping Matthew's dad's hand. "Lydia, looking great as always . . ."

I had no idea what that little exchange was all about, and at that moment, I didn't care. I could've killed them both.

Becky took a few more steps until she reached a hallway wall, then leaned back against it, still staring down.

I pushed through a few more people to get to her. "What's up with all that?" I asked her, shooting a useless glare at her parents. They were still busy gushing over Matthew, who looked uncomfortable and dismayed at the attention.

"Clients," Becky whispered.

"What?"

"Don and Lydia Quince are Mom and Dad's clients," she said to the floor. "That's why they came tonight."

"Your parents?" I said, still totally lost. "You mean they didn't . . ."

I couldn't make myself finish the sentence. *You mean they didn't come to see you?*

"Becky . . . god, I'm sorry," I said.

Becky didn't look up. Just nodded distantly.

"You were awesome," I told her.

She made no move. The newsboy cap shaded her eyes. I was tempted to touch her chin, get her to lift her face, but I didn't. After a moment, Becky raised her head and shrugged.

"Thanks," she said carelessly. "Glad you thought so."

She sounded casual, unaffected by her parents' attitude, but I couldn't believe it.

"You want to get out of here?" I asked, just as my cell vibrated in my pocket.

Cursing, I checked the screen. A text from Sydney.

WE WON FIRST PLACE!!!

"Crap," I whispered. I started typing back, and while I was doing that, Becky suddenly launched herself off the wall and tore through the crowd, making a beeline for the classroom serving as the girls' dressing room.

"Shit!" I said as I finished my text: *Cool good job glad to hear it*

Hands landed on my shoulders from behind me just as I sent the message. "Dude, that was awesome!" Gabby said into my ear.

I barely got turned around before she wrapped me in a hug. Mom and Dad appeared, waving and smiling, and grouped up on my sister and me so that we were in a standing dog pile.

"That was tremendous!" my mom said.

"Great show, Ty, great show," Dad said.

"Thanks," I said, still strangled. They finally let me go but blocked my path.

"You guys have a great department this year," Gabby said. "No kidding. I thought it was just going to be like our little shows, but whoever's running the department now really knows their stuff."

"That's Mrs. Goldie, yeah," I said, trying not to keep too conspicuous an eye on the dressing rooms. "She's great. The actors are really good, so . . . that helps."

"Oh, yeah!" Gabby said. "They really tore it up!"

Mom glanced around at the crowd. "Where is Sydney?" she asked. "I thought she'd be here tonight with you."

"Debate tournament," I said. "It was a qualifier for State. She'll be back later. They won, though."

"Oh, wonderful!" Mom said.

"Not surprised," Gabby said.

Before they could go off on how remarkable my girl-friend was, I said, "I need to start on our lockup, so I'll see you at the car?"

"Sure thing," Dad said, patting his pockets for his keys. He does this twelve times per minute; it's kind of funny. "We'll be waiting. Let's go, everybody."

Mom gave me another hug, and Gabby punched me rapid-fire in the ribs. Not hard. Then they shuffled through the crowd and out of the building.

Since I couldn't very well go into the actresses' dressing

room to see if Becky was still there, I moved back into the auditorium to start doing our final lockup. It took maybe ten, fifteen minutes, whereas during the last week of rehearsal, it had taken me twenty. I may have been rushing the tiniest bit.

When I got back to the hallway, the place had cleared out except for a couple of actors lingering with their families.

I didn't see Becky's parents, or Becky, anywhere.

"Hey, did Becky come out yet?" I asked Ross, who was talking with Mrs. Goldie.

"Um . . . couldn't say, man. Hey, good work tonight, by the way."

"Thanks, you too. Listen—"

"Oh, Tyler!" Mrs. Goldie said, giving me a school-district-approved side-hug. "Ross is right, you were simply marvelous. Nice job!"

"Uh, thanks, but listen—"

"Did you do an idiot check on the lobby?" Ross interrupted. "Idiot check" was a slang term for triple-checking to ensure all the doors had been locked and everything valuable put away, that kind of thing. There were plenty of students with sticky fingers wandering around during school hours.

"No, not yet," I said, giving up my quest to ask them for more info on Becky's whereabouts. "I'll do it now."

"Cool, thanks. Hey, you coming to the cast party Saturday?"

"I can't *heeeear* this!" Mrs. Goldie sang with a laugh, and went into her office. Cast parties, I'd been told, had nothing to do with Masque & Gavel. Only students who'd been involved with the show got invited, but the parties weren't official in any way. I'd also heard they were way more insane than the parties held by other students. It was hard to tell facts from rumors around the department, though. Freshman year, I'd heard that all the guys were black belts in karate. And that some kid once dressed up like the Phantom of the Opera and ran around the auditorium in the dark. And that—well, you get the idea.

"I hadn't . . . no, I didn't plan . . . I mean, I don't know," I said to Ross.

"Well, you should," he said. "It'll be a rager. I'm gonna get wiped *out*."

I wondered if Becky would be there. "Sure, yeah," I said, just in case. "I'll be there."

"Cool."

I headed back into the auditorium to do my idiot check on the lobby doors and the booth. The only lights left on now were work lights high above the stage. The set cast shadows in every direction. An empty auditorium, even with the house lights on, can be a creepy place, no doubt about it.

I jogged through the auditorium, checked all the doors, then made my way back toward the stage. Movement in the stage right wings—the spaces just offstage—caught my eye. Not wanting to be stuck there any longer than I had to, I started to move in that direction to tell whoever it was that we needed to vacate.

And stopped dead.

The stage manager had a tall stool to sit on during the show so he could see over everyone's head onstage and call up cues to Ross and me in the booth. Becky was sitting on that stool. I could only see her profile. She still wore the newsboy cap and the rest of her costume.

But the straps on her overalls were undone and hanging by her hips, the bib rolled down to her waist. Her head was tilted back, her eyes closed. The off-white button-down shirt she wore under the overalls was open.

She wore nothing beneath that. I could see one small point of her star tattoo.

And Matthew Quince/Atticus Finch was in front of her, his face buried in her chest. The sounds I heard, the noises he made, grabbed my intestines and wound them around a splintered wooden spool.

I hadn't made a sound, but Becky's head suddenly turned toward me, her eyes open. Matthew didn't seem to notice. Guess I didn't blame him.

We locked eyes, Becky and me. For a thousand years.

I waited for her to push Matthew away. Or tell him to stop, at least.

She didn't.

Just looked at me looking at them.

I took a backward step, quiet. Then another. Then turned and hurried out to the hallway. I didn't know this for sure, but I felt like she watched me every step of the way.

By the time I got to our car a few minutes later, I was

en*raged*. I knew it was stupid, but it was like, how could she do this to me? And the obvious answer was, she *wasn't*. We weren't together. She could do whatever she wanted. With whoever she wanted.

"All set?" Mom asked as I got into the backseat beside my sister.

"Yes," I snapped.

"Whoa, Tyler," Dad said, starting the engine. "Did you blow the place up by accident or something?"

"Let's just go."

Mom frowned, looking over her shoulder at me. Gabby's face was surprised too.

"Hey, Dad was kidding," Mom said. "What's wrong?"

"I don't wanna talk about it. Can we go?"

"Was it the show?"

"No, Mom, it wasn't the show, the show was fine, can we leave, please?" I dug the heels of my hands into my eyes, wishing for steel wool to abrade the image of Becky and Matthew from my corneas.

"Okay," Dad said. "We're outta here."

I wanted to scream, wanted to punch Matthew dead in the face. I could've buried that tall sucker.

"What's up?" Gabrielle whispered.

I shook my head.

The parking lot was almost empty. Just as Dad was backing out of the parking space, I saw Becky come out of the drama department. She didn't see me, and she didn't know what kind of car Dad drove. She got into the driver's seat of a blue Jeep Liberty SUV, shiny beneath the parking lot lights. She'd changed into her regular clothes.

Briefly, through my rage, I wondered how in the world she was allowed to drive. She was fifteen too, and couldn't have gotten more than a permit to drive with another licensed adult. I didn't see anyone in the car with her.

When Dad drove past her, she didn't even look up. She just put both hands on the top of the steering wheel and rested her forehead between them.

I almost told Dad to stop. To go back. That there was someone I needed to talk to.

Almost.

Dad turned on the radio as we pulled out of the lot. I guess I'd brought the whole fam down, because no one said a word. I did see Gabby getting and sending text messages for a bit, but that was all.

Gabrielle scowled at her phone. "Give me your cell," she said.

"Why?"

"Now."

Because older sisters always win no matter what, I tossed her my cell. Gabby began texting real fast, eyes narrow in the pale light of the screen. After a minute, she tossed it back into my lap.

"There," she said. "I just bailed your ass out."

I looked at my outgoing messages. The last one was to Sydney.

Hey sorry my last text was short had stuff to do. You are awesome! I knew you'd do great. Congratulations, Syd. I'll take you out for dinner to celebrate. :)

"The hell's this?" I said to Gabby.

"Her team won first place," Gabby said. "And you're all like, 'Hidey-ho, whatever, nice job, have a neat summer.' *God,* you're dumb sometimes."

Oops. While I couldn't bring myself to thank Gabby out loud—my mind was still mostly elsewhere—I did have to acknowledge that she probably just saved me a whole lot of trouble.

"What are you guys talking about?" Mom asked.

"Nothing," we said together.

A few minutes later, about halfway home and only mildly back in my right mind, I asked everyone, "You'd tell me if I did a bad job, right?"

Mom turned. "Bad job at what, sweetie?"

"In the show. I mean, if the lights sucked, or the stage went black or something. You'd tell me, right?"

"If the stage went black, I think you'd know," Dad said.

"Okay, what if I was an actor, and I totally sucked? You'd tell me, wouldn't you?"

Mom winced. "No," she said carefully. "I don't think we could ever say you sucked."

"Even if I did?"

"No," she said again. "Even if you did, we'd still be proud of you, and we'd tell you so. At the absolute worst, it still takes a lot of guts to get up in front of people and perform. And, Tyler, we *are* proud of you, being so involved like this. We both think it's been really good for you."

"Yep," Dad said. "Absolutely."

I hadn't known that. I forgot about Becky for a nanosecond. "How so?"

"It got you away from your computer," Mom said, glancing at me with a grin. "Not that we want you to stop writing, of course. We're both proud of that, too. But your mood has definitely been different coming home from school after rehearsals. Lighter. More . . . smiley."

Well, that was an easy one to explain. Not that I was about to try.

I wasn't surprised by her response, either. It was nice to hear, obviously, but not a shock. Mom and Dad were pretty attentive to me and Gabrielle both. Irritating, yes. But kinda nice.

"You want to tell us what's bothering you?" Mom asked as we stopped at the last streetlight before our neighborhood.

"A friend of mine is in the show," I said. "And her parents didn't even congratulate her. Just went on and on about this other guy because his parents are their clients or something."

"What kind of clients?"

"I don't know. Doesn't matter."

"Well, that *is* obnoxious," Mom said. "How'd she take it, this friend of yours?"

"She seemed okay, but I think it hurt her."

"It did," Dad stated, moving the car through the green light. "I guarantee you it did."

Mom nodded. "That's ridiculous," she said. "You should've pointed her out to us so we could give her extra lovin's."

I snorted at the dumb phrase. *"Extra lovin's," huh?*

Was that what Matthew had been giving Becky?

six

. . . . .

I sit down on the short wall delineating the grass from the parking lot, switching my cell to my other ear. "Mom and Dad again, huh?" I ask Becky. "What happened?"

"I don't know," Becky says. "Just everything."

"What can I do? Name it."

Becky is quiet. I don't push. I've learned over the last year it won't get me anywhere. So I sit and wait, wishing for the first time in my life that I smoked so I'd have something to do.

"I don't know where else to go," she says finally.

"Go?"

"I mean . . . I don't know."

"Becky, if you want me there, I'm there. You know that."

"Yeah. Thanks."

Another long pause.

"You gotta talk to me," I venture. "I'll sit here on the phone all night if you want me to, or I'll come over, or bring you a freaking gallon of Ben and Jerry's, or whatever, but I can't help if you don't tell me how."

"Ben and Jerry's only comes in pints, Sparky."

"Then I will fly to Vermont and make it happen by brute force and naked aggression."

Becky sniffs. Such a small sound, but it hurts so much. It's like a laugh, but not.

While I think dumbly, *I just said "naked" to Becky Webb, huh huh huh huh!*, Becky says, "Tell me about the magazine."

. . . . .

I didn't talk to Becky in the two days after opening night of *Mockingbird*. Didn't even look for her. Went to the booth, did my job, went home. That Friday morning before school, Mom asked me about "the little girl who played Scout." I passed on that one.

I didn't explain that the "friend of mine" I'd talked about in the car on opening night was Becky, didn't want to point her out as the girl who needed "extra lovin's." What was a cute euphemism for encouragement from my mom became an ironic dagger in my belly when I thought of what Matthew had done opening night.

On closing night, Ross asked again if I was coming to

the cast party. I hadn't intended to, not after the Matthew thing. But when he asked, I said, "Yeah, I am. Could I get a ride?"

"I can get you there, yeah," Ross said. "But you might want to find another way home. No way am I driving anywhere!"

I sent a text to Gabby first to see if she'd mind picking me up.

Sure, she wrote back. *You drinking?*

No, I wrote.

Good man. Sydney coming with?

No, I wrote.

She didn't write anything back after that. Sydney probably could have come, but technically since she wasn't involved in the show, she didn't get an invite.

I managed to wait until after the curtain call to ask Ross if Becky was going to the party. Ross grunted and grinned. Beneath the red glare of the booth lights, his face looked wicked.

"I hope so," he said.

I didn't like the sound of that. "How come?" I asked.

Ross didn't even glance at me. "Just . . . stick around," he said.

When we'd finished our idiot check—I'd lost track entirely of Becky, which was partly on purpose because I was still fuming—Ross drove me and a couple other techies to the party. The entire cast and crew were there, and nearly everyone was drinking. Ross fetched me a beer from a cooler, slapped it into my hand, and said, "Don't do anyone I wouldn't do!"

"Right, got it," I said. "Hey, whose house is this, anyway? Is it cool that we're here?"

"Matthew's," Ross said, and my stomach twisted. "Yeah, it's cool. His parents go out of town all the time. See ya!"

With that, he abandoned me for the backyard, where most of the cast had migrated.

I opened the beer and took just enough of a sip to convince anyone looking that I was, in fact, drinking the thing. It tasted awful. I spent ten minutes kicking back against one wall, nodding and saying hi to people who passed by and congratulated me on my first tech experience. This included, of course, Neapolitan Girl.

"So where's Syd?" she asked as she walked by with a cigarette in one hand and a bottle of beer in the other.

"Friends," I said.

"You didn't invite her?" she asked. She sounded surprised.

"Was I supposed to?"

The girl shrugged. "You *could've*," she said. "That's all."

"Oh," I said. "Um. Next time."

"Cool!" the girl said, and wandered off.

Matthew's house. I couldn't have dreamed of a worse place to be. And I hadn't even seen Becky anywhere. The only reason I'd shown up was to—I don't know. Yell at her? Beat up Matthew? Not a clue. Just seemed like the perfect bad idea at the time to agree to come.

Restless, I moved out to the backyard. Kids were gathered in groups, mostly laughing, a few groping. When I spotted Becky, I almost dropped my beer.

She sat by herself by the swimming pool, her legs dangling in the water. She had a beanbag chair stuffed under her back and took long, practiced hits off a small blue pipe. I could tell by the way she held each inhalation what she was smoking.

I wanted to rush over and knock the pipe into the pool. *Stop!* I screamed in my head. *What are you doing, you don't do this, stop!*

Okay, so, it's not like this was a moral issue for me. If someone wanted to get high from time to time and deal with frying their brains, more power to 'em. But not Becky.

I mean, it wasn't that she was smoking out; it was how easily she was doing it. No hesitation, no uncertainty. Think about a fifth grader sneaking his first cigarette in the alley versus a pack-a-day addict—you can tell by body language who has been doing it longer.

This wasn't an experiment for Becky, and it killed me. It wasn't who she was supposed to be.

I set my beer down on a lawn table, went back inside, and texted Gabby.

Ready to go.

I expected her to text back. Instead, my phone rang. I didn't want to answer it, didn't feel like dealing with Gabrielle's big-sister bit.

I hit the button anyway. "Hello."

"What happened?"

"Can you just . . . I'm just ready to go."

Gabby paused. "On the way," she said finally, and hung up.

Sometimes having a sibling means not having to say anything.

I went out front and waited for her. Gabby showed up in less than fifteen minutes, driving her ancient red Honda. I got in and slammed the door shut.

My sister said, "So . . ."

"Whatever," I snarled.

Gabby let the car roll down the street. "Easy there, peaches," she said. "What happened?"

"Why did you get high?"

Gabby laughed. This improved my mood not at all. She trailed off when she saw I wasn't enthused by her reaction. "Well," she said, "I guess because it was fun. Yeah. Final answer."

"You did it a *lot*."

"I wanted to have a lot of fun."

"Have you done it since Mom and Dad busted you?"

Gabrielle shrugged. "You itching to try it out? Or have you already?"

"I tried it a couple times last year with Robby and Justin."

"So what did you get into tonight?"

"It's not me, it's . . ."

Gabby lifted her eyebrows but didn't take her eyes off the road.

"Okay, look," I said, "if I tell you something, you have to promise not to tell Sydney."

"Ohhhh-kay. Pinkie swear."

"Okay, so, on the first day of school last year . . ."

I unwrapped the entire Becky saga as it existed at that point. I barely registered that when I concluded the story with what I'd seen tonight, we'd been sitting in her car in our driveway for at least half an hour.

"I see," Gabby said when I stopped talking. "So, couple things. First, are you saying you don't like Sydney anymore?"

"No, it's not that. I do like her," I said. "She's great. But Becky's . . . I don't know . . ."

"Becky is unattainable," Gabby said. "And I can't help but wonder if that's part of the attraction."

"It's crossed my mind, but I don't think so," I said. "There's just something about her. . . ."

"Something about the way she takes off her clothes for guys and gets high."

"That's not who she is!"

"But it's what she does. What else defines a person?"

"That's not all there is to her," I said. "She's—"

"Broken."

I scowled at my sister. "What?"

"Ty, listen, there's doing dumb things in high school because it's high school," Gabby said. "Drink, smoke, ditch, whatever. But there's something else going on with this girl, and whatever it is, you don't want any part of it. Trust me." She opened her door and put one foot outside. "You got a

116

great girl in Sydney. This Becky chick is bad news, I promise you. I mean, crushes can be kind of fun, but don't let it mess up the good stuff you've got."

"But I can't stop thinking about her," I said.

"So write a story about it," Gabby said. "Use it for inspiration." She reached out and shoved my shoulder. "I got homework to do. Lock it up before you come in."

She got out and closed the door. I watched her go inside, then sat alone in the passenger seat of the Honda for a while.

Write a story about it? Yeah, did that. But I figured another couldn't hurt. So I went in and got to work.

With my job as lighting operator over, I swore off any more drama club meetings, despite a few techies and actors stopping me in the hall or talking to me in classes we shared. They were nice and all, but nothing could scrape the image of Becky and Matthew from my head, or of Becky poolside at the cast party.

These elements did not make it into the story I wrote over that weekend. If anything, my character Becky grew more perfect.

But I avoided the real thing at school.

I spent more time with Sydney than I had during the weeks of rehearsals, and Sydney asked no questions. She seemed happy I wanted to hang out with her more often. Before too long, we'd be hitting the one-year mark. A whole year. I don't know how she put up with me. Or why. I guess Gabby was right—I was lucky to have her.

I returned to writing short stories, mostly melodramatic

crap and some horror stuff. I went to a How to Get Published seminar at an indie bookstore and started sending out short-story manuscripts to as many magazines and websites as I could—horror stories and one particular version of my many Becky stories. I'd finally settled on what I thought was the best version of it, and I only sent it out in hopes of killing off my desire for her. Kind of like throwing out photos of an ex-girlfriend.

I sent it to about a dozen different magazines in the week following the cast party. The magazines that bothered to respond at all weren't interested.

Yet.

●　　●　　●　　●　　●

"It's no big deal," I say to Becky. "It's a short story for this magazine called . . . *Blood Tales.*"

"*Blood Tales?*" Becky repeats, and I'm pleased to hear her voice clearing up. "That's graphic. What's the story?"

"Uh . . . buncha guys turn into werewolves and eat a girl alive. Basically."

Becky gives me an appreciative laugh. "Awesome. Are they paying you?"

"Eh, a few bucks."

Blood Tales is paying me fifty dollars, to be exact, but I don't want to say it. On one hand, fifty bucks isn't going to pay the rent, as my dad would say. On the other hand, it was the first story I'd sold, and fifty was better than nothing; it was fifty more than most aspiring writers make. I'm thrilled, to be honest. I just don't feel like broadcasting it. Most people don't understand how hard it is to sell a story. I've got a stack of rejection letters to prove it. Sydney, Robby, and Justin know, but only because I explained it.

Also, there's one more thing I don't want to tell Becky. *Can't* tell her, not yet.

It's the first time I've ever lied to her.

I did get a story in *Blood Tales,* and it was about werewolves, and it did pay fifty bucks, which I am still waiting to get in the mail. But that's not why we're out here tonight.

It's not why *I'm* out here tonight.

I'm out here tonight to celebrate another story altogether. In another magazine. The very one my mom gave to Sydney earlier this fine evening.

Maybe you've heard the story. It's about this guy who has fallen hard for a girl he can't have? Yeah, that one.

Two copies of the magazine where the story appears arrived this afternoon in my mailbox—my only form of payment. "Contributor's copies," they call it. Which means I won't get paid cash, but the magazine—*The Literary Quarterly Review*—has more readers than *Blood Tales*. It's a nice credit to have. It's a well-respected magazine, and to have been accepted at my age is rare, I'm pretty sure. Probably won't hurt my college applications, either.

My copy of the magazine is in my car right now. Under the driver's seat. I have plans for it. The other copy *had been* in Mom's hands. *Until.*

No way in hell am I going to let anyone else read it,

though. While there's nothing libelous in the story—I did a lot of research on libel before I submitted it—anyone who knows me even remotely will put the pieces together before the end of the first paragraph. Kind of like Sydney did.

"Still," Becky goes on. "A few bucks is a few bucks. That's what you always wanted. I'm proud of you."

I get a strange lump in my throat when she says it. "Thanks. So listen . . ."

Headlights sweep across me as a car pulls into the parking lot. A little white Sentra.

Sydney's little white Sentra.

". . . Um . . . can I call you back?" I say.

"If you want," Becky says. "No big."

"Cool. Give me fifteen minutes. Okay?"

"Sure."

"Hey, Mustardseed . . . you gonna be okay?"

"Aren't I always, Sparky?"

She hangs up.

I do not like the way she said that. Defeated.

Sydney parks her car next to mine and fast-steps toward me. I put my phone in my pocket.

"Hey," I say when she gets to me.

"Thank god," Syd says, and gives me a quick hug. My arms automatically hug her back, even though I'm shocked at her attitude. I was expecting a knife in the eye, or worse.

"I thought maybe you were already out there on the street somewhere," Syd says.

"I'm not hammered," I tell her.

"No . . . I guess not," Sydney says. She tilts her head, looking over my shoulder at the picnic table. The guys call out to her, but it doesn't sound like they're headed our way.

"So what's all the drama with your little manic pixie dream girl?" Sydney says, sitting beside me on the wall.

"My what?"

Sydney reaches into her back pocket and brandishes Mom's copy of *LQR*. I fight the urge to scream and yank it from her hand. I don't want creases in it.

Syd waves the folded magazine in my face. "Manic pixie dream girl," she says. She uses her Masque & Gavel–approved jazz hands for emphasis. "The adorably eccentric sweetheart who dazzles a broody male lead?"

"I have no idea what you're even saying."

"Yeah, you do." Syd crosses her legs and flips the magazine open, right to my story. "Rebecca Webb," she says. "You were talking to her earlier. What's going on?"

Damn. "I don't *know* what's going on."

"I don't believe you."

"Not my problem."

She closes the magazine and holds it in one hand. "You're being a real ass tonight, Tyler."

As usual, she doesn't sound angry or whiny or bitchy when she says this. It's just a statement of fact.

Maybe Syd's right—I *know* she's right—because all I can think about is how I can get her the hell out of here so I can call Becky back.

And maybe it's the last bubbles of alcohol talking, but it

hits me that sometimes, there's just no time like the present to get something over with.

"Syd . . . why are you out here?"

She bumps her shoulder into mine. "Because I was worried you were drinking and driving. I went to two other parks before I found you."

"No, no, I mean . . . why . . . why bother?"

"I just said I was worried about you."

The oblique approach is clearly not working. I try to come up with exactly the right words to do this. I gaze out across the parking lot because I can't look her in the eye when I say what's coming next.

"I'm in love with Becky Webb."

I sense Sydney staring at me.

Then she bursts out laughing.

. . . . .

"All right, my academicians," Ms. Hochhalter said on the Friday one week after *Mockingbird* closed. "One quick announcement, and then we're into *Fahrenheit 451*. Mrs. Goldie in the drama department announced yesterday she's looking for original one-act plays to produce for the spring show."

I sat up straight. Sydney cast me a *Did you hear that?* glance.

"So if anyone has any interest in submitting a play, come see me after the bell and I'll give you the list of requirements.

122

Get it, got it, good. Now, *Fahrenheit*. Do any of you malefactors even know who Ray Bradbury is?"

I didn't hear a single word anyone said the rest of class, although I was a fan of Bradbury. I still hadn't written more than a few pages of some dumb plays, and that was a long time ago, back when Syd had first brought up the idea. But I figured I could still whip something up. After class, I was the only person who took a copy of the submission requirements from Ms. Hochhalter, photocopied on a sheet of pink paper.

"Ah, I wondered if you'd be interested, Tyler," she said when I asked for the sheet. She handed it to me and smiled. "I'd love to read anything you come up with."

"I'm not a hundred percent sure I can," I told her, scanning the sheet.

"He will," Syd said from the doorway, where she was waiting for her post-English-class kiss.

Still looking at the sheet, I went over to Sydney. She fell into step beside me as we went to our next classes.

"Hang out tonight?" she asked.

"Uh . . . homework," I said.

"Tyler, why not just say, 'No, Sydney, I'm going to be writing a play.' It would really save time and effort."

I finally looked up, and grinned. "Sorry," I said. "Yeah, that's probably what I'll be doing."

"That's cool. Good luck with it."

"You're not mad?"

"Sure I am," Sydney said, acting offended. "But I can't complain too much since the whole playwriting thing was kind of my idea in the first place."

"True."

We reached her biology class. Syd leaned in and kissed me. "Call me, though," she said. "Just for a bit, okay?"

"Totally. What're you going to be up to?"

"I don't know. Probably call Michelle and Staci, see if they're up for something."

"Okay. Cool. See ya."

I turned to go, but Syd stopped me.

"Tyler. You're good, you know that, right?"

"As opposed to evil?"

"Mmm . . . no, you're a little evil . . . just a dab."

"Just a dollop?"

"Just a pinch." She smiled at me. "I mean at writing. You're really good. And you really should do this playwriting thing. It might be good for college applications and stuff."

I laughed. "Ah, screw that, we're sophomores!"

I was joking, more or less, but Sydney didn't laugh with me.

"Not forever," she said, and with another quick kiss, disappeared into her class.

God, Syd. I stood there for a moment, lingering on both her kiss and her words. Sometimes she just sounded way too mature. There are people like Robby and Justin, who cruise through high school, sucking up every moment, every good and bad day, taking it all in. Then there are people like Sydney, who act like high school's just a speed bump. A four-year slog they have to suffer through before getting on to the business of real life or something.

Maybe I fell somewhere in the middle, because as I turned the corner, headed for chemistry, I was already considering and instantly rejecting a hundred different play ideas. I didn't think about college, but I wasn't thinking about high school, either.

Which is maybe why for the first time in my life, I forgot who else used this particular hallway at this particular time of the day.

"Hey, Sparky!"

I stopped short as Becky appeared in front of me, holding her books against her chest.

". . . Hey."

"Where ya been all week?" Becky asked.

I stuttered uselessly. Where had I been?

Avoiding Becky Webb, that's where. Now, *there* was a fresh and original idea.

Until the thing backstage with Matthew and her, I'd always taken this route to my next class. Since Monday, I'd taken another hall specifically to avoid her.

"Around," I said.

Becky squinted at me. "Are you mad at me?"

"No."

"You look mad."

Here's what I did not say:

You're goddamn right I'm mad! What were you doing with

that tall assbag backstage after the show, huh? Letting him get all over you like that. You're not even dating! Are you? Tell me if you are, so I can stop spending every waking moment thinking about you, okay? Could you do that for me? I would give anything to kiss you, to hug you, and instead you let some senior jackass maul you like that? Thanks. I thought it hurt last year when I couldn't even talk to you, but now we're friends, and I get to sort of hang out with you sometimes, which is more than I'd ever hoped for, but let's face it, that'll never be enough, and, you know what, never mind, I clearly can't be around you without feeling like total shit, so have a good life.

Here's what I did say:

"I'm fine."

I must've been convincing, because Becky tugged on the paper in my hands. "This the play thing?"

"Um . . . yeah."

"Are you writing one?"

"Thinking about it."

"Well, write me a nice big part, okay?" She kicked my shoe. Which practically made me drop everything in my hands, grab her, and give her the most cinematic kiss ever imagined. So much for staying mad.

"I'll try," I said.

"Cool. See ya, Sparky."

She went on down the hall, and I watched her go as I always did, unable to keep myself from admiring her walk, her clothes, her everything.

Then I headed toward chemistry, re-hating Rebecca

Webb's guts for how she treated herself, and thus, by extension, me.

But not really.

What's your deal, dude? I thought, not worrying at all about making it to class on time. *You love her, you hate her, which is it?*

It wasn't jealousy, though I was jealous. It wasn't anger, though I was angry, mostly at Matthew.

No, it was the fact that I didn't really know her; that's what hit the hardest. That I didn't and couldn't understand why she'd done it.

My short story hadn't sold to the *Literary Quarterly Review* at this point, and I'd stopped sending it anywhere else. Walking in the hallway that day, as the final bell rang for class, I realized I'd created a character not just for the story, but for Becky, too.

Never mind what I knew or thought I knew. Since our friendship was loose at best, I was free to daydream about who I *wanted* her to be. I took her body and wrote her emotions, cares, worries, sense of humor, goals, and dreams the way I wanted them to be. Some I transcribed to paper. Most I kept to myself.

Letting Matthew suck on her like that, practically in public, shamelessly; her smoking out at the cast party . . . those were not part of who I needed her to be.

When I got home that afternoon, I made myself a vanilla milk shake and fired up my computer. By the time I was getting ready for bed at midnight, I'd finished the first draft of a one-act play about a guy and a girl who wake up to find that they're the only survivors of a global plague, and that they've mysteriously become immune to all forms of illness and aging.

At 12:03, I got a text from Sydney.

No call huh? Okay talk to you tomorrow then.

I didn't respond. I turned on my radio, low, and got in bed, trying to decide if I should even bother submitting the play to Mrs. Goldie. The sheet Ms. Hochhalter gave me said that after Mrs. Goldie selected the plays, the casts would be chosen from among the Drama Two students.

Which meant Becky.

Which meant if my play got chosen, there was a chance she'd be in it.

Which meant I might end up working with her on another play, in close contact, because the playwrights were expected to work with Mrs. Goldie and the student directors she picked out.

I wasn't sure I was ready for that.

But why had I bothered to take the sheet from Ms. Hochhalter in the first place, then?

Yep.

· · · · ·

"What the hell's so funny?" I say to Sydney as she continues laughing.

"You!" she says. "God, Tyler! Is that supposed to be a news flash? Let me post that online so the whole world will know you're in love with Rebecca Webb. Oh, wait—the whole world *already* knows."

I scowl at her. "What?"

"Oh, for Pete's sake," Sydney says, shaking her head now. "Even Mrs. Goldie knows. Everyone knows. You're the worst actor in the known universe, Ty. You may as well buy ad space on every billboard in the city."

Believe it or not? This is news to me. I thought I'd done a great job of hiding it since Sydney and I had started dating.

"Okay, fine. Then let's circle back to the whole 'Why are you here?' question. Why are you sitting here right now if you know that? Why are you even with me?"

"Hey, I could ask you the same question, bucko."

Good point.

"Just answer it," I say.

Sydney sighs. "Because, Tyler," she says. "You're a great guy, and I'm lucky to have you. And I guess . . . I dunno, I guess I was holding out hope that someday you'd get over her and be with me for once."

"I've been with you since freshman year."

"You've been around me," Sydney says. "Not with me. You know that. *I* know that. I bet Robby and Justin know it too. Want to go ask them?"

I hear Justin's telltale cackle echoing through the park at something Robby said.

"No," I say.

"Do you want to stop? Me and you?"

". . . I don't know," I say. Except—I do.

"Ty," Sydney says, "I really like you. Even though you're an idiot about this whole Rebecca Webb thing, it's almost kind of cute, and I—"

"Hang on, why does that make me an idiot?" I say, standing. "What's so dumb about it? So I have a—an unrequited love or whatever, so what? Why is that *cute*? To *you*?"

I really want her to get mad. Stomp around, scream, cuss. But Sydney's businesslike demeanor doesn't shift an inch.

"Because you don't know her," Sydney says.

"Oh yeah? What don't I know?" I am getting really pissed now. I can't even say for sure at who, or what.

"You don't want to know," Sydney says, like I'm a child. "That's the point."

"So tell me!"

"Hey!" Robby shouts. "Everything okay, you little loveberries?"

"Just a second!" I scream at him. Justin, naturally, laughs. It's a sound I am rapidly tiring of.

I turn back to Sydney. "Well?"

"Tyler," Syd says gently, "Becca Webb is always—"

"Becky," I correct her. "Becky, or Rebecca. Why does everyone call her Becca?"

Sydney coughs, which sounds to me like a chuckle of disbelief, rubs her forehead, and goes on.

"Rebecca Webb is, to put it politely, always open for business. And the fact that you love her from afar when she'd

gladly put out for you is just sort of funny. I mean, you have a pulse and a penis. That's about all it takes."

"Shut up!"

What's left of the grin on Syd's face evaporates.

My vision tints red. For the first time in my life, I want to take a swing at someone. Anyone.

"That's petty, drama-class gossipy bullshit," I say. "And no matter what you and me had, or don't have, or whatever, I never thought you'd cop to that kind of shit. It's pathetic."

Sydney, unperturbed, stands and folds her arms. "You asked," she says. "And I'm not the pathetic one in this equation."

I whip away from her and stalk into the parking lot. I don't know where I'm going or what I'm going to do, but I want to hurt something. Bad.

Because when all is said and done . . . she's right.

seven

· · · · ·

I turned the script in to Mrs. Goldie first thing Monday morning. She acted thrilled, but then, I figured she's the drama teacher: of course she's acting.

Turned out she wasn't.

"She loved it!" Sydney said when I met her by the parking lot after school. "Mrs. Goldie is totally picking your play, Tyler!" She hugged me tight.

I hugged her back, surprised. "Oh," I said.

Sydney pulled away and laughed. "Well, don't have a heart attack from excitement," she said. "Aren't you happy?"

Over Sydney's shoulder, I watched Becky getting into her Jeep and maneuvering out of the lot. The first step was over; now all I had to do was see who was going to be cast in my show.

"How many plays did she end up picking?"

"Three, probably," Syd said. "All I know is yours is one of them. She hasn't picked the others yet."

"When is she casting?"

"Probably by Friday. Rehearsals start after Christmas break. Oh, she also wanted me to ask if you were up for running lights again."

Becky Webb notwithstanding? I couldn't get away from that damn drama department! At least, that was my first thought. After a couple seconds, though, I realized I didn't mind. Robby and Justin and I hung out all the time, and I had Sydney, of course, but it wasn't like I belonged someplace. Maybe now I did.

"Maybe, yeah," I said.

I spent the rest of the week alternately dreading and anticipating Mrs. Goldie's casting choices. I also opted for my normal route to chemistry. I couldn't resist the opportunity to at least see Becky. We said hi to each other, but not much more. I thought the tension between us was practically visible, hovering in the muggy air of the school corridor, but I couldn't tell if Becky felt it too.

When Syd handed me Mrs. Goldie's cast list on Friday, I didn't know whether to be disappointed or relieved. Becky was not in my show.

"Does Mrs. Goldie still want me for lights?" I asked Syd as I studied the list.

"Far as I know," Sydney said.

"Cool," I said. "Tell her I'll do it."

Why? Because I couldn't bear not talking to Becky anymore. I wanted our *Mockingbird* friendship back. If it was all I could have, then I'd take it. Except I didn't think I could attempt it without getting the foulness of Matthew Quince out of my head. I at least had to know why she did it, if they were dating or what.

But what if they weren't? Had I really seen what I had backstage that night? God, what if I'd gone bonkers and imagined the whole thing?

Then I realized, if that was true, Becky would have said something to me about virtually ignoring her the past week. It was hard to explain, even to myself, but I knew instinctively that she'd merely let me keep my distance, that it was up to me if I wanted to make a production out of it.

And I sort of wanted to.

So later that day, on the way to chemistry, instead of saying hi as we passed, I flagged her over to one side.

"Hey, Sparky," she said, smiling.

I froze up.

"Hey," I said back. "Listen, I . . . I thought maybe we should get together sometime—hang out together, I mean—and talk?"

I hoped she'd guess what I meant so I wouldn't have to spell it out. *I need to talk to you about what I saw you and Matthew doing, because it really bugged me and I miss you and you're better than that and I wish it was me not him. . . .*

Maybe not in those exact words.

"Totally," Becky said. "When?"

I hesitated again, completely disarmed by her friendliness, her willingness, her *I don't have a care in the world what you saw* attitude.

"Um . . . whenever," I said.

"You want to come by my place?"

I thought the sidewalk had dropped out from under me.

"I'm sorry?" I said.

"My house," she said. "Do you. Want to. Come over. After school today."

Shocked, suspicious, scared, grateful, I said, "Yeah, okay."

"Cool. Meet me by the drama department after sixth hour."

"Yeah . . . okay."

"Great. See ya there."

She walked off down the hall.

That simple? I thought as I floated to class. Really that simple? This whole time?

I wasn't under any misconceptions, like we were going to hook up or anything; this was strictly a platonic hangout. But damn, if I'd known it was so easy, I would've asked her to hang out a long time ago!

And if I had . . . where might we be by now? What if I'd talked to her earlier, before Sydney had asked me out?

What *if?*

I failed a chem quiz, heard nothing anyone talked about

at lunch, and took no notes in American history. I was, to put it mildly, preoccupied. I wrote a thousand stories in my mind about what could and should happen at Becky's house.

But by the time school was out, I'd started running through a number of worst-case scenarios: she wouldn't be waiting for me; Sydney would intercept me on the way; Matthew would be coming along too . . .

None of which happened. After sixth hour, I practically ran to the drama department, and I found Becky leaning against a wall, her black leather backpack dangling from one hand.

"Ready?" she asked as I approached.

"Um . . . yeah!" I said.

"Well then, we're off." She led the way through the escaping student body to her car.

The Jeep smelled of vanilla, though I didn't see a car freshener anywhere. It wasn't overpowering, but it still made me dizzy. I don't think it had anything to do with the scent itself, of course.

"Nice car," I said.

"Thanks. Mom got it for me."

"Damn! Rough gig."

Becky paused before turning the ignition.

"Sometimes," she said.

I left it alone.

"You got a car?" she asked.

"Nope. Permit, though. I might be able to borrow my

mom's car after Christmas. I'm hoping to start driving to school next year."

"Do it. There's nothing better."

"Are you, um . . . I mean, you're fifteen, right?"

"Yeah?"

"So how did you get a license?"

Becky smirked and shifted into drive. "Who says I have a license?"

And she stomped on the gas, barreling out of the parking lot and onto the street, narrowly avoiding a school bus. She giggled at the near miss.

Becky turned on her stereo. A prehistoric U2 song came on the radio, something soft and mellow. Good choice; it helped my heart slow down. It was still thudding from the peel-out, and from being in her car. On the way to her *house*.

Based on the house Becky drove us to, and remembering her parents' clothing at the play, it was clear her family was—well, I wouldn't say filthy rich, but they did pretty well for themselves. Her house wasn't a mansion, but it was in an older part of town with bigger property lots.

The white exterior blinded me as we pulled up. The yard, landscaped in precise detail, had no leaf out of place. Sterile. The driveway didn't have a single oil spot or crack; I couldn't imagine how that was even possible. Gabby and my dad parked in the gravel along one side of the garage because there was only room for Mom's car inside.

"Okeydoke," Becky said. "Welcome to Casa de Webb. *The den of iniquity!* Come on in."

I left my bag in her car and followed her to a pair of front doors inlaid with glass and crystal prisms. We went in, and I couldn't help raising my eyebrows at the chandelier in the foyer. The hall, floored with dazzling white tile, opened on the left into a huge sitting room, sporting a tan leather couch and dark wood furniture. But no TV, just a liquor cabinet and some weird-ass art on the walls.

Becky led me past this room, and I caught a glimpse of a very modern kitchen, also to the left, all blacks and whites and chromes. I didn't think anyone ever actually prepared food in it; nothing was out of place, no cereal boxes lined up on any counters or smudges on the stainless steel fridge. Straight ahead lay another living area, showing off a high-def TV about as wide as Becky's car was long.

"Holy . . . ," I said, walking into the TV room. It was dark and plush, with room enough for a small party. I stood by the black suede couch, taking in the details. A redbrick fireplace was recessed in one wall. Several framed photos lined the mantelpiece.

"It's no big," Becky said behind me.

"Clearly, you're not referring to the TV," I told her.

She snickered, which made me feel good. I'd almost forgotten I was there to talk to her about the Matthew thing.

But talk about what, exactly? I couldn't decide. Mostly I wanted to find a way to be able to talk to her again like we used to. I couldn't figure out how to do that without bringing up how it felt to have caught them the way I did. Which would by necessity include telling her how much I cared about her, which could end up getting back to Sydney, who, I assumed, believed my days of crushing on Becky Webb were over.

I moved toward the fireplace to look at the photos. Becky as a baby. Some young guy with her color hair. Becky in a soccer uniform, early grade school. The same young guy in a high school baseball uniform.

"Who's this?" I asked, pointing to the guy. He looked like an all-star something or other.

"Ugh. William. My brother. He's a cocksucker."

"Literally?"

"Don't know, don't care. He's a jerk."

I almost snapped my fingers when I realized where I recognized him from. This was the guy who'd sat beside her last year in the cafeteria. Not a boyfriend, not even a student—her big brother.

"I saw him at school once last year, right?"

I thought I saw Becky's shoulders tense. "Yeah," she said in a sharp bark. "Like I said. Jerk."

I fell back into step behind her as she walked down a long, tiled hall toward her room. "Why's that?"

"Because he told me the truth."

"Doesn't the truth set you free?"

Becky stopped cold and whirled on me. "No, it doesn't," she snapped. "It just makes you go ass-over-elbows crazy in the head."

I am so dumb.

"Sorry," I said.

Becky rubbed her eyes. "No, I'm sorry," she said. "It's not you. He told me Mom and Dad were planning on getting a divorce because of me, but because of work they had to stay together, and that as soon as I graduate, they'll finish the job. That's all."

That's all? I thought. *What a messed-up thing to tell someone.*

"What do you mean, 'because of you'?"

"He's my *half* brother," Becky said.

"Your mom was married bef— Oh." Call me Captain Obvious.

"Yeah," Becky said. *"Oh.* See, according to William, Mom had a little romp with the pool boy, or the tennis pro, or the mailman . . . whatever porn cliché you want to choose. And a few *wakachicka wakachicka*s later, enter little old me."

"Did you ask them if it's true, though?" I said carefully. "I mean, if he's a jerk, maybe—"

Becky spit out a laugh void of any trace of merriment. "Ask them?" she repeated. "I don't have to. They have separate goddamn bedrooms. When they're both here at the same time, that is. Which is, oh, once every *never.*"

"Why do they stay together? I mean, if they have separate rooms, that sounds serious. People get divorced all the time with kids involved."

Becky pursed her lips. "Ready for this?" she said. She

lowered her voice, as if imparting a great secret. "It might cause a scene at the club."

"What club?"

"The country club," Becky said. "Golf, tennis, that kind of thing. Dad plays the former, Mom plays the latter. If they got a divorce now, people would *talk,* don'tcha know. Can't have that. Not yet, anyway. See, it'll be easier on their precious professional and social lives to pretend like everything's fine until I get out of here. That way they can be seen as brave and caring for sticking together for the sake of their younger child. You know, the one with the *problems.*"

I had no idea what to say after that. *What problems?* I screamed in my head. You can't have any problems—you drive a new car at fifteen without a license, you live in a swank part of town, you're talented, you're beautiful . . .

The Matthew thing, that was a mistake, a—an error in judgment, that's all. We all made mistakes, right? Didn't we?

"They've both got clients there," Becky said, probably in response to the confused expression I wore. "Lots of clients, lots of money. A divorce could ruin all that, at least at the moment."

"What do they do?" I ask as we continued down the hall.

"Hell if I know. Insurance or something."

We reached her bedroom door. She opened it and went in.

She opened her *bedroom* door. For me. I could barely breathe.

Becky tossed her backpack on the floor and paused to yawn and stretch. When she did, her midnight-blue shirt lifted up an inch or two, and the small ribbon of skin I saw made my eyeballs spin. I'd have given anything to touch her there. My god, it was just her *waist,* but it was killing me.

Not wanting to get myself into any more trouble than I already was, I began studying her room, which mine would have probably neatly fit into, memorizing its every texture, its every essence. The walls were off-white, with a black-bladed ceiling fan above. A smooth, polished desk sat pushed into one corner, with a row of books neatly lined above it. One was the old copy of *Night Shift* I'd seen her reading that first day in the cafeteria. The desk matched a bureau and vanity along the opposite wall. She had an attached bathroom off one corner. Her bed—a queen, I thought—was covered with a floral-patterned comforter.

Becky flopped onto her bed and began massaging her scalp. "So, this is it," she said. "We have *arriven.* What's on your mind?"

Not daring to sit beside her, I chose her black leather swivel desk chair instead. "Huh?" I said.

"You wanted to talk about something?"

"Oh!" I said. "Yeah. Right. Well. I guess . . ."

She pulled her legs up and crossed them on her mattress, turning to face me more squarely. I swear, the look on her face . . . . she had no idea what I was going to say.

Which made two of us.

"Are your parents home?" I blurted out.

"Nah. Dad'll be by in a bit, probably. Maybe."

"He sells insurance, huh?" Quite suddenly, I did not want to bring up Matthew at all.

"Sells it, buys it, trades it, embezzles it, takes it out for drinks . . . I dunno, couldn't tell ya."

"How about you, you any good at math?"

"Probably."

I laughed, but she didn't.

"Hey, you're in Honors English, aren't you?" she asked.

"Yeah," I said, trying to conceal my surprise that she knew this about me. "Are you?"

"Heh. No," Becky said, rolling her eyes. "I'm an *exceptional student.*"

I knew what she meant: she was in the Exceptional Student Program, which, despite its name, was basically for all the burnouts, idiots, and losers of the school. Dumbed-down classes. I'm just calling it what it is, okay? Ask Justin; he'd been in those classes since freshman year, and he'll be the first to admit it's where all the dumb kids—who aren't dumb enough to drop out—end up.

And she didn't belong there. How could a student perform the lead role in a play as well as she did and yet be thought of as stupid?

"Really," I said. I didn't want to sound as shocked as I was. Fictional Becky wasn't dumb, and I didn't think Real Becky was either.

"That's what they tell me," Becky said. "Kind of a misnomer, don't you think? 'Exceptional'?"

143

See, that's what I meant. A dumb kid wouldn't use a word like "misnomer."

"I've always thought so," I said.

"It's a *hoot*," she said.

"I don't think you belong there," I said.

"You don't? How's that?"

"You're not stupid."

"Stupid has little if anything to do with it, Sparky," she said. "It has everything to do with . . ."

She stopped herself and bit her lip. Damn. Shoot me. If I was a tenth as debonair as my fictional characters, I would have eased her down on the bed right then and there. Alas, I was only me.

"With?" I asked, praying my jeans were concealing where my mind was headed.

"With what you can get away with when no one's looking."

The phrase was loaded, I could feel it, but I couldn't tell how. Then it hit me.

"Like getting high."

"Sure," she said. "For example."

I don't know what my expression revealed, but Becky squinted at me and added, "Does that bother you?"

"Not— I mean, it just surprised me, is all."

"Why?"

Because you're perfect, I thought.

"Because you're different," I said.

"Am I, now!"

I shrugged.

"Don't you ever want to just forget about everything for a while?" she asked.

"Sometimes."

"Well, if it makes you feel better, I only do it on very specific days, okay?"

"What days?"

"Days that they're looking for it."

I started to push the question, but Becky laughed—whether it was to herself or at me, I couldn't say—and spoke again before I could.

"So how do you do it?" she said.

"Do what?"

"Forget about everything for a while."

"Oh. Write, I guess."

"One-act plays?" she asked, wriggling her eyebrows.

"That was my first," I said. "Mostly I write . . . stories. . . ."

Uh-oh. Didn't mean to say that. What if she asked me—

"What do you write about?"

Danger! Retreat! What the hell had I gotten myself into?

"All sorts of things, I guess."

"That's cool," Becky said. "You never said anything about that before. Can I read some of it?"

I could've laughed out loud. "Um, yeah, sure," I said. I could always dig up one of my old horror stories or something, I figured. And as terrified as I was, with her coming so close to finding out what—or who—I generally wrote about, having her ask me to read something made my breath go shallow.

Her door was still open, and through it, I heard the front door open and close. The *click-clack* of business shoes against the white tile in the foyer. Very adult noises. My day-dream of lying beside her on her bed ended abruptly with me getting gut-shot with a single blast of her father's pearl-handled .45 pistol I conjured just for the occasion.

I tensed. Becky grinned.

"Don't worry, it's just my dad," she said.

"It's okay that I'm here?"

She held up a finger. "Hi!" she called through the open door.

I heard things being set down, keys jingling, the fridge being opened. No response.

Becky raised her eyebrows at me. "See?"

"Oh," I said. "Okay."

But then I heard his heavy, leather-clad feet clacking. Headed this way. I got nervous all over again.

"Chill out, Sparky," Becky said, and stretched casually out on her bed. "It doesn't matter."

I almost begged her to sit up. Her relaxed position—T-shirt creeping upward just an inch—gave the impression we'd been up to some bit of naughtiness and I'd just leaped to the desk chair to avoid looking guilty.

Didn't she have any idea how the scene would look to her father walking in? That my life was in mortal peril?

Mr. Webb showed up in her doorway, riffling through mail. Again in a suit, again looking almighty and powerful.

He gave me the briefest nod in the history of dismissals, and said to Becky, "Did you make up that test in math?"

"Nope," Becky said carelessly.

"Why is that?"

"I'm failing everything anyway," she said, running her fingers through her short hair. "So I'll probably drop out, go live on the street somewhere."

"You think this is real funny, don't you, Rebecca."

"Don't you see me laughing?"

Mr. Webb snorted. "Fuck you," he said, and went back down the hall, re-riffling his mail.

The room became an igloo, all ice and chill. I stared at the empty hole of her doorway, seething and scared. Scared of what, I wasn't sure. Possibly of what I was considering doing to that asshole with my bare hands.

"Told ya," Becky said, and flipped over onto her stomach. Suddenly, she buried her face into her pillow, fists gripping it and pressing it up over her ears, and screamed. *Screamed.*

The sound tore me in half. My first, most base instinct was to go to her, but I didn't.

After a few minutes of breathing heavily, while I sat there being silently stupid and useless, Becky pulled herself back up to a sitting position, her face splotched red. I was glad to see there were no tears in her eyes.

"Anyway," she said, and blew bangs off her face. "What was it you wanted to talk about?"

"Are you really failing everything?"

"That's why you wanted to talk to me? To ask about my scholastic achievement? Gotta say, Ty, that doesn't exactly get my motor running."

"But are you?" I persisted. Because in my stories, she was a straight-A student. Possibly valedictorian. It was part of her perfection.

"Maybe not *failing*," she said. "I mean, I do need Daddy to pay for college, right? Somewhere out of state. I'll be fine."

She winced when she said it. Slightly, but it was there.

"So that's our big talk, huh?" she said.

"No, um . . . I just wanted to ask you about . . ."

As I tried to find the words to confront her about Matthew, I realized I'd already decided I didn't want to know after all.

There was nothing to be gained. Even if I asked her if they were dating, so what if they weren't? Would I ask her out, then? No. It was too risky now. I was *in her bedroom,* for god's sake, and I wanted to be invited back.

". . . about whether you think I should stick around the drama department," I finished.

"Totally," Becky said. "You did great. And everyone really likes you."

But why don't they like you? I wanted to ask, but didn't.

"Okay, cool," I said. "Thanks."

Becky slowly smiled at me, tilting her head, giving me a quizzical look. I had no idea what she was thinking. Suddenly, she shook herself, like she'd been chilled.

"Well, that wasn't so bad," she said. "You want a ride home?"

. . . . .

I walk back to the wall, where Sydney has resumed sitting. Beyond her, at the table, Justin is trying vainly to win an arm-wrestling contest with Robby.

"You don't know the first thing about Becky," I say to Sydney.

"But you do?"

"I know enough."

Sydney shrugs. "Okay. What do you want to do, then? Are we done here?"

"Hey, I didn't invite you to come scouring the city park system for—"

"No, I mean, are *we* done, Tyler."

"It doesn't look like that would upset you."

"Would it upset *you?*"

"I don't know." I pause. "You can do better."

"Wow, thanks," Sydney marvels. "You want to break up to save my poor soul from you?"

I don't reply.

Sydney stands back up, comes to me, and takes my face in her hands. I start to resist, then give up. Sydney puts a single, gentle kiss against my lips. It's not unlike putting on your favorite sweats in the middle of winter—warm, comforting, and familiar. Even though you know they're threadbare, full of holes, and on the verge of disintegrating.

"I'm going to do you a favor," she says, still holding me, forcing me to look into her eyes. "I'm going to break up with you right now. Done. Snap. It's over. See, that wasn't so bad. But I'm telling you, Tyler . . . your 'love' isn't going to be enough for her. Hear me?"

What am I supposed to do, say yes?

"She can only hurt you," Sydney adds. She gives me another kiss, this time on the cheek. Her hands drop from my face. "I at least never did that."

I can't argue that point.

"I'll make it easy for you," Sydney says, pulling her keys out of her pocket. "Don't call. Don't text me. Don't come over. We'll see each other Monday, and we'll be civil, and that'll be that. Okay?"

I nod slowly. The reality of my new situation is not sinking in very quickly.

"Okay," Sydney says. "Take care of yourself." She waves at the table. "Bye, boys!" she calls.

Robby waves. Justin cries out, "Later on, Pink Floyd!"

Sydney stops. "Okay, what's up with the Pink Floyd thing? Every time I ask—"

"They just laugh," I finish for her. "One of the founders of the band was named Syd Barrett."

I say this even as I'm still trying to ascertain who and where I am now without her.

"Oh." Suddenly, she giggles. "Oh! Really? Wow. Who knew?"

Sydney draws one finger beneath one eye. Nothing more. She tips her head backward. "See ya in English."

Without waiting for a response, she walks back to the white Sentra, climbs in, and drives out of the parking lot. It occurs to me she still has the magazine.

I have the decency to wait until I can no longer see the car before calling Becky.

It's almost midnight.

eight

· · · · ·

"Did I ever tell you your girlfriend wants to kick my ass?"

It was the fourth or fifth time I'd been to Becky's house since rehearsals for the one-act plays started. I was on her bed—let *that* little bit of info sink in for a moment—with my back against her headboard, chowing on a bowl of microwave popcorn while she sat at her desk working on a book report for her English class. The book? *To Kill a Mockingbird.* She *had* to ace that one.

I choked on a piece of popcorn skin. "Say what?"

Becky tossed a wry grin over her shoulder at me. "Well, okay, maybe that's overstating it. She said to stay out of her way."

"When did she say that?" I demanded. I reached for my phone to call Sydney and yell at her.

"Oh, man, this was the first day of school," Becky said, twisting her hips in the chair to swivel it back and forth. "She walked up to me out of nowhere and said, 'I'm going out with Tyler Darcy now. I'm asking you as a friend to please stay out of my way.'"

"Wow. Sorry." I stopped reaching for my phone.

"No big. I didn't even know who you were."

Ouch. Stabbed. Still—I was sitting on Becky Webb's *bed.* Life could be worse. Who cared if she didn't know me then? She knew me now.

"Is that why you talked to me that day?" I asked.

"Yep. If I was going to get into a catfight, I wanted to know who it was over."

We both laughed at the idea. Sydney wasn't the catfight type. And—this was strange as hell—it was kind of cool Syd was concerned enough over stupid me to even say something like that to Becky.

"Funny thing is," Becky said, "I didn't even know we were friends until she said it. Me and Sydney, I mean. She talked to me in drama, when we had to work together, but that was it."

"Weird."

"Yeah. I mean, me and you didn't even know each other."

Becky typed a new sentence. Her report was almost done. I watched her, noting every crease of her clothing, every arch of her fingers. The silence was comfortable, which thrilled me. We didn't always have to be talking. I took that as a very good sign. And I guess—well, I guess that's why I didn't spill my guts. We were friends. I was in her room. We talked, we laughed. If I opened my big idiot mouth now, it could ruin what I had. *Better to remain silent and be thought a fool* or whatnot.

"So, what do you like about her?" Becky asked.

I swallowed a handful of popcorn and tried not to choke again. "Sydney?"

"No, Sparky, the queen of England. Yes, Sydney. What do you like about her?"

Of all the conversations on planet Earth we could have, this was the absolute last one I wanted. "Well," I said, trying not to sound like I was weighing my words too much, "she's—"

"And you can't say 'nice'!" Becky said.

"—fun," I said.

"Fun how? Like, go to the sock hop fun, or graphic porno sex fun?"

I tried very hard to force a laugh and couldn't. Didn't seem to matter; Becky wasn't laughing either.

"Uh . . . somewhere in the middle," I said. I put the popcorn bowl aside. Wasn't hungry anymore.

"Are you happy?" Becky asked.

"Are you asking me or are you running lines?" Her character in the one-act she was in, Jill, said that line several times during the show.

"Asking," Becky said, turning the chair to face me. "Although, I probably should run lines, too."

"At this particular moment in time, I'm extremely happy," I said. Which was the truth. More truthful, in fact, than she could know. I chose the words deliberately, I think, to see if she'd catch my implication.

But Becky only nodded thoughtfully. Over her shoulder, I could see her computer screen and the title of her book report. *To Mill a Kockingbird*. I had to smile at the intentional misspellings. Then wondered if they *were* intentional. Then called myself an idiot for even wondering.

"Are you?" I asked. "Happy?"

"For the most part? No. Not especially." She shut one eye as the after-school sun poked through her window and lit up one side of her face. Sunlight traced gold along her profile, like she was the fairy queen Titania herself. "But at this particular moment in time, it's all good."

I wanted to take my meaning of the same phrase and lend it to hers. So badly. That she was as happy to be here with me as I was with her. But I just couldn't tell if she meant it the same way or not.

Her parents' voices trickled in from the kitchen. Low tones. No joy. Keys jingling. Heels clacking coldly on the tile.

"Are they headed out?" I asked. Because every time we were here alone, I couldn't help but wonder if one of my myriad dreams about Becky was going to come true. They never did, though. .

Becky shrugged. "Let's find out." She yelled toward the open bedroom door, "Bye, see you later, have fun tonight, I love you!"

The noises in the kitchen didn't change. Her parents didn't respond. A minute later, I heard them at the front door, which opened and boomed closed a second later.

"Does that answer your question?" Becky said, and turned back to her computer.

I didn't know which question she was referring to: whether she was happy, or whether her parents were leaving.

But I could guess.

Becky hit two keys on her keyboard simultaneously, then a third. The book report highlighted, then disappeared. She saved the empty document and closed the program.

"Easy F," she whispered, and twirled carelessly in her chair. "Wanna run lines with me?"

. . . . .

Once Sydney's car is out of sight, I call Becky back.

"Hi," she says when she picks up.

"How you doing, Mustardseed?" I ask, starting to make my way back toward the table.

"Swell."

I stop about halfway to the table. "Becky, what happened tonight? This isn't just some random crankiness at your parents. Talk to me."

"My mom hates me."

"Becky, come on."

"Well, let's see. I said, 'I need my permission slip signed for the next show,' and she said, 'Ask your father,' and I said, 'But he's not here and you are,' and she said, 'Well, that's just fucktastic,' and I said, 'You shouldn't swear in front of your children,' and she said, 'Rebecca, shut up. I hate you.' So . . . yeah, think that settles it."

Goddamn it.

"I'm sorry," I say.

"Don't be. I could've tossed out the whole 'He's not my real dad' routine, but that sounds so trite, don't you think?"

I wish I could laugh.

"You know what I did almost say, though?" she goes on, and her pace picks up. Like she just can't get it out fast enough. "I did almost ask why she bothered, why she even bothered having me, I mean. Why not just abort me when she had the chance, right? I mean—"

She's spinning out. I've never heard her like this. "Becky, stop . . ."

"—why even go through all the pain and turmoil and expense of a kid when you can just dump it? Right? Why'd they even bother, huh?"

"Stop, stop, please." She's killing me.

Becky takes a sharp breath. There's silence for a few moments. Then she lets the breath out and takes on a fake chipper tone.

"Right. Sorry about that. Got a little carried away, huh? So, where are you?"

"Still at the park." I stop for a second, catching my breath. *Shit,* that outburst really scared me.

But when she asks me, as if everything is perfectly fine, "You okay there, Sparky?" I say, "Yeah, good. I just broke up with Sydney," so that I won't have to tell her why I'm really sounding breathless, and then I realize what I just said and that it's for real.

"Wow," Becky says. "That's a big step."

It *is* a big step, but I'm not sure how Becky means it.

"Was it because I called?" Becky asks.

I think about this. Heart rate returning to normal now. "No," I decide. "Not really. No."

"What was it?"

"It was time. That's about it."

"Fair enough. You all right?"

"Yeah. I'm fine. No big. So what now?"

"What now what?"

"What're you going to do, what can *I* do, what's going on . . . ?"

"I don't know, man," Becky says. "I don't know. I'd go to bed but I'm so not tired. I want Starbucks."

"Everything's pretty much closed or I'd bring you some."

"Aw. You're sweet."

I love/hate when she says things like that.

"I think I'll just take a shower and read or something," Becky goes on. "Stay the hell out of any other room in the house. Ponder the mystery of the universe or something."

"Are you alone?" I ask, and wince. What I should have

said was, *Are either of your parents home?* My phrasing makes it sound like I'm asking if there's some guy there with her.

"At the moment," she says, which doesn't exactly calm me down.

"I can bring you ice cream," I say.

"Tyler," Becky says, "you are my bestest friend in the whole world."

· · · · ·

The one-act plays turned out awesome. Better than *Mockingbird,* in many ways. Becky's show, called *Jack & Jill & Bill & Phil,* was a farce, I guess, with a lot of mistaken identities and double entendres. I hadn't realized how great her timing was until the performance. She had the audience roaring.

My show, *Prophet,* felt like kind of a bummer, because between Becky's show and the third one—another comedy—mine wasn't exactly hysterical. Humor wasn't my thing. Still, I suppose the fact that no one laughed is a *good* thing; the audience sat quiet and still throughout the performance, no one yawning or shuffling in their seats. Plus, the actors got a great round of applause during the curtain call. And watching this girl Amy deliver *Prophet*'s final monologue about how the end of the world can also be a beginning . . . yeah, it was cheesy, but I have to admit, I loved seeing it brought to life. And Pete—the guy who'd almost killed me during *Mockingbird*—did a great job directing my play.

I ran lights for all three one-acts. Since it was my second show with the department, I had a lot more fun; I knew my way around, I knew the other people involved—the girl with Neapolitan hair was named Danielle, it turned out—and I knew what I was doing, sort of, with the lights. I wouldn't have predicted that it would be something I enjoyed, but I really did.

After the show on opening night, I made sure I was in the drama department hallway when Becky came out of the girls' dressing room. She'd already changed her clothes. I didn't see her parents anywhere.

"You want to get out of here?" I asked.

We'd spent our breaks during rehearsal together often, just like during *Mockingbird*. Talking about this teacher, that teacher; this class, that class; this music, that music. Once she wore a blue Just This Once T-shirt with the *Black Cymbal* album cover printed on it. I downloaded the album that night and played it till I liked it. I did not tell her I did this, or tell her I remembered the logo patch safety-pinned to her freshman-year bag. I hadn't even known for sure it *was* a band till she wore the shirt.

"Yeah, let's," Becky said. "You want to go to my place?"

Of course I did. I couldn't imagine why she wanted me there, but I wasn't about to argue.

"Sure," I said.

I was hesitant to go back into the auditorium to do the idiot check, terrified that when I came back through, I'd find her with Matthew again, who had played the lead opposite

Becky in her show. But when I got back to the hall, Becky was there waiting for me, off by herself.

Relieved, I smiled at her, and she smiled back. Then I paused when I saw my sister racing toward me from the end of the hall, dodging all the family and friends gathered to congratulate the cast.

Crap. Forgot about this part.

"Hey!" Gabby cried, and wrapped me in a big hug. Because she's my sister and I love her, I hugged her back. That didn't mean I wasn't surprised.

"Uh . . . hey," I said. "What're you doing here?"

"Seeing your show, dumbass," Gabby said, letting me go.

Over her shoulder I saw Becky sigh silently, duck her head, and turn to leave. No way I was going to let that happen.

"I know Mom and Dad are coming tomorrow," Gabby was saying, "but I've got that class—"

"Becky!" I said, cutting Gabrielle off. "Hold up. This is my sister, Gabrielle."

Becky paused, and both she and my sister turned at the same time, facing each other. The look on Gabby's face would've cracked me up if this situation hadn't, you know, involved me. The look said, quite clearly, *So you're the notorious Becky I've heard so much about.*

"Becky," Gabby said. "Hi. It's, um . . . so nice to meet you."

She said it with a pleasant look on her face, but I'd known my sister fifteen years, and she was scanning Becky like a goddamn Terminator. Not that she didn't like Becky, exactly. Just . . . checking her out.

"Nice to meet you, too," Becky said quietly. To me, she said, "So, I'm just going to head out. I'll see you tomorrow."

"Wait, no," I said. "I thought we were going to hang out."

Gabby made a show of clearing her throat to get my attention. She threw a hitchhiker thumb over one shoulder. "I left Sydney in the restroom," she said. "She'll be here in just a minute."

". . . You brought Sydney with you?"

"She wanted it to be a surprise," Gabby said. She paused. "Surprise!"

"I really should go," Becky said. And maybe it was my imagination, or maybe it was only what I wanted to see, but I swear she looked disappointed.

"Wait a second," I said. "You don't have to—"

"Hey, Tyler, congratulations!" Sydney said from behind me.

I spun around. She gave me a big hug, then a kiss, which I returned on instinct, and her hand slid down my arm to take mine.

"Hey, Becky," Syd said, sounding friendly enough, but definitely not releasing my hand. "You were *so* great in that show."

Beside us, Gabby snapped her fingers. "Wait, you were in that first one, right? The Fred and Bill and Jack thing?"

"Jack & Jill & Bill & Phil," Becky said. "I was Jill."

"Right!" Gabby said. "You were hysterical!"

And like with Syd, I couldn't tell if my sister was being sincere or not. I think she was. And I think Becky felt it too, because she finally smiled a little.

"Thanks," she said, and looked at the floor.

"So, now what?" Sydney said. "You guys want to get something to eat?"

Damn.

"I was just heading out," Becky said, oddly repeating the exact same thumb-over-the-shoulder gesture Gabby had used.

Too much was happening way too fast. A checklist raced through my brain:

1. Becky invited me to her house. At night. Good!

2. Sydney is here, so that's not going to happen. Bad.

3. But she just invited Becky to go out to eat with us, like it's no big deal, and that's really cool of her. Good!

4. Sydney didn't exactly specify Becky by name, so maybe she didn't mean to include her, and Becky's probably not going to want to go anyway. Bad.

And just when things couldn't have gotten any weirder, two hands crashed down on my shoulders. God, I kept getting ambushed!

"Well, look at this gorgeous grouping of humanity!" Robby shouted. Robby has no "indoor voice."

"Rob? Hey, man . . . what're you doing here?"

"Came to see your show, dude!" Robby said, moving to join our circle. Justin appeared next to him from the crowd, looking vaguely pissy.

"It was awesome!" Rob said, then lowered his voice. "And who was that chick at the end? Is she around? 'Cause, *man.*"

Slow down!

That's what I wanted to scream at the top of my lungs, to everyone in the hall. Everything was happening too fast, way too fast, and someone was gonna get hurt.

"We were just talking about going out for some food. You want to come?" Syd asked my friends.

"Food? Uh, hello," Robby said. "The trash compactor scene in *Star Wars*? Little-known fact: filmed in my stomach."

"Actually, I have no earthly clue what you're talking about, but point taken," Syd said, and laughed. So did Gabby. She thought Robby was hysterical.

Normally, I did too. But Becky was already slowly side-stepping away from the group, blending into the crowd.

"Becky," I said.

"I should get going," she said quickly. "Get home, you know."

Watch carefully as I took masterful control of the situation by stating, "I thought we were going to hang out."

To what shall I compare the silence that followed? Oh, the hallway was loud and bustling, as always after a performance. But our little group turned to ice.

The thing was, it wasn't an accident. I said it on purpose. And I said it for one simple reason. I was standing there surrounded by my sister, my girlfriend, and my two best friends. Becky was surrounded by no one. And that, for me—for me *and* how I felt about her—was utter bullshit.

"Well . . . ," Becky said softly, eyes darting to Syd.

Syd locked her eyes on me. But if she was mad, she didn't show it. Actually, mad might've been better.

"You . . . made plans with her?" Syd asked.

"Kind of," I said.

"*Kind* of," Syd repeated.

"Look, I didn't know anybody was coming tonight," I said. "Maybe if I'd known, we could've done something else."

"Oh, brother," Gabby sighed, and I didn't know if she meant it in a sibling way, or just to avoid cussing.

Sydney searched my eyes. For what, I don't know.

But Becky had stopped inching away and stood watching Sydney and me now.

Syd stared up at me for another few moments. "Okay," she said finally. "That's . . . cool." She looked at my sister. "So. *Coffee?*"

It came out pointed enough to stab flesh. Gabby nodded quickly. "Oh yeah, uh-huh," she said.

"Sounds good to me," Robby crowed, apparently missing the drama swirling beneath the discussion. "Where at?"

"Um, I think this is a girls' night out," Gabby said, squinting one eye toward me.

"Oh," Robby said. "Bummer. Well, does anyone know where that girl— There she is! Hey! Hi! I'm Robby!"

He was off, smashing his way through the crowd.

Justin, who'd barely moved this whole time, rolled his eyes. "Sometimes, I just wish we could go to a bar," he muttered. "See ya later, man."

"Later," I said as Justin squirreled between people to keep up with Robby.

"So, um . . . I guess I'll just . . . wait out front?" Becky said to me, like she wasn't sure I was really going to show up there.

"Yeah," I said. "I'll be there in a minute."

Becky nodded. "No problem." She started to go, then stopped and turned to Syd. "Thanks for coming," she said. "Seriously. I mean, I know you were here to see Ty's show and everything, but . . ."

"Sure," Syd said. "I mean, yes—you did a great job, Becca."

Becky inhaled sharply, eyes blazing. Then the look vanished. "Right," Becky said. "Understood. I mean, thanks. I meant to say thanks. Yeah. So. Bye."

"Bye," Sydney said.

"Later," Gabby called.

When Becky had gone, I faced Sydney. "Look—" I began.

Right then, Robby came plunging back into us, smiling. "Got her number!" he said. "Hell. Yeah. How're you kids holding up?"

"Well, I don't think I've ever been more embarrassed in my entire life," Sydney said, looking at me.

"Wait a second," I said. "We're just going to hang out, that's it."

166

"Were you planning on telling me you were hanging out with her?"

"I didn't know until just a little while ago."

"Yet the question stands, Tyler."

Robby slid over to my sister and folded his arms. "Shoulda brought a camera to capture this tender moment," he stage-whispered. Gabby shot an elbow into his ribs.

"Why don't you ask me *why* I'm hanging out with her tonight," I said to Sydney.

"Okay, why?"

"Because she doesn't have anyone else. Have you ever met her parents? They're . . . well, god, they're assholes. They're not like yours, or mine. And they're not even here. I feel bad for her, Syd, okay? And we're just hanging out, that's it."

"Yes, you keep saying that, almost too much, really," Sydney said.

Robby slipped an arm around Gabby's shoulders. "Gabrielle," he said, "would you ever consider dating a younger man?"

"Younger man? Yes. Boy child? No."

"That hurts me. Deeply."

"Something else is gonna hurt if you don't get that arm off me, Robert," she said. Laughing.

"Syd," I said, wishing Gabby and Robby would take their chatter elsewhere, "I'm sorry if I did something to hurt you or embarrass you. I never meant to do that. But I seriously had no idea you were coming tonight."

"And that would've changed things?"

"Absolutely."

"Do you know any other girlfriend on earth who would let you get away with this?"

"There's nothing to get away with."

That seemed to do the trick. Sydney shook her head a little, then pulled me in for a kiss, which I returned.

"You're a jerk," she said.

"Yes, but also drop-dead sexy."

Gabby raised a hand to her mouth as if to whisper to me. "Don't push your luck," she said, *not* whispering.

I reached out and gave Syd another hug. "I'll call you tomorrow," I said. "Or I can call you when I get home tonight, even."

"It's okay," Syd said. "Tomorrow's fine."

"Okay. I'll see you all later."

"See you at home," Gabby said, drilling me with her eyes. She took Syd's hand and walked her out of the hallway.

Robby and I watched them go.

"That," Robby said, "was the most profound scam in the history of the world. Nicely done, dude."

"What scam?" I said. "I was just being honest."

Robby eyed me as a surprised look flashed across his face. "Oh," he said. "Really? Wow. Okay."

"Really, yeah," I said. "I gotta go."

"Sure thing," Robby said. "I'm gonna call that Amy chick."

"Uh . . . she's right down the hall, man."

"I know. But this way is funnier. And like, cute, you know?"

"Whatever you say, Rob."

"Hey, man."

"Yeah."

"You really just gonna hang out? That's really it?"

"Almost certainly."

"Huh." Robby shook his head. "You're a strange man. Catch ya later."

He went off the way the girls had gone, while I went the other way, the way Becky had left. I found her sitting on the sidewalk of the parking lot, in the same place she used to wait for her rides. I sat beside her.

"Ready?"

She nodded but didn't look at me. "Would you like a side of awkward with that?"

"I'm sorry," I said. "I didn't know they were coming, and—"

"No worries."

Pete and Ross walked past, headed for Ross's car. "Later, Ty," Ross called, and Pete said the same.

I raised a hand to them. "Okay, I gotta know," I said to Becky as they got into Ross's car. "Why the hell does everyone in this department act like you don't exist?"

Becky shrugged. "It's no big."

"Well, it's irritating," I said.

"Don't lose sleep over it, Sparky. Let's go, huh?"

We got up and walked to her car, which still and always

had a trace of vanilla aroma in it that drove my whole body mad. I'd been to her house several times by then. Always after rehearsals, never on a weekend. Mostly I helped her work on her lines.

Which is to say, just for clarification, we did nothing even remotely resembling a date. We didn't watch or go to movies, or eat together, or hold hands—much less make out. I guess by that point, because of all the time we were spending together at and outside rehearsals, we'd gotten to be better friends. The Matthew thing seemed ages ago.

Whether Sydney knew how much time we were spending together or not, I couldn't've said. Fortunately—*he said sarcastically*—Becky was keen to find out.

"So . . . ," she said as she drove us to her house, "are you sure your girlfriend doesn't mind this?"

Nothing tasted more bitter than when Becky pointed out I was, in fact, dating Sydney. Pissed, though not exactly at Becky, I stabbed back, "I don't know, what's 'this'?"

How's that for passive-aggressive? I couldn't help it. I didn't know what "this" thing was. We weren't hooking up; we weren't doing anything besides what normal friends *do*. And . . . that sort of sucked.

My tone wasn't lost on Becky, who gave me a surprised glance. "Hey, man," she said. "I was just asking. I don't want Sydney to ground you or something, put you in a time-out."

She elbowed my arm and offered a smile. Which I accepted. Of course I accepted.

"I don't know if she minds or not," I said. "Because

other than tonight, I haven't exactly told her. But she hasn't asked, so."

"Okay, you know that won't help your case if she finds out."

"No. Why are you asking, by the way?"

Becky shrugged. "I mean it; I don't want you to get in trouble with her. That's all. But I don't know her well enough to know if she's one of those girls who gets mad about her boyfriend having friends who also happen to be girls."

Stop calling me that! I thought. *Don't call me her boyfriend!*

Even if it was true. I couldn't stand hearing it spoken with Becky's voice.

"She has friends," I added, though I didn't know why. "I mean, she has people she hangs out with. She has a life."

Becky laughed out loud. "I didn't ask *anything* like that!" she said. "Holy Saint Francis, defensive much?"

I pulled on a smile, but it didn't fit right.

"What do you think of her?" I blurted out, then wished I hadn't. Then didn't care. Then wished I hadn't again.

"She's okay," Becky said, and gave me a look when I laughed. "What?"

"Nothing, you're right, she is," I said. "I just don't know what that word means. Do you?"

"It means she's not an unrepentant bitch," Becky said. "So that's something."

We both laughed at that. Part of me felt bad for doing so. Which, by definition, means a part of me did not.

When we got to Becky's house, I followed her back to

her room. Since we were a lot closer these days, I again sat on her bed instead of taking the chair.

"So, now, what's up with people not talking to you ever?" I asked.

"Why don't you ask your girlfriend?" Becky said. And her tone was so measured, I couldn't in a million years figure out the subtext.

But I didn't like the way it sounded.

"How come?" I said.

Becky smirked at me. "I'm going to take a shower," she said.

"Are you dodging the question?"

"Hmm. Yes. Pretty much. Yes. Going to shower now."

"Yeah, okay," I said.

I started to get up, to leave her room, you know? Go wait in the kitchen or something.

But before I could even get my feet under me, Becky walked into her bathroom without a look back.

And without shutting the door.

I could see her shadow—cast by the light over her sink, which was hidden around the corner—spilling out onto her carpet. From where I sat, I could see a foot-wide strip of the bathroom wall, and her robe hanging from a hook there.

What I could *hear* . . .

What I could hear was each centimeter of fabric being pulled away from her body. Her shoes being removed and tossed back into the bedroom, her socks peeling off one after the other, the zipper on her jeans drawing down—

172

I could have moved just a half foot to my left to get an actual glimpse of her. It wouldn't have been hard at all. And I mean, she left the door *open*.

But I didn't move. I was as still as a frog pinned to a dish of black tar, flayed open for evisceration.

A few moments later, I heard her shower curtain sliding open. The creak of the faucet being turned. Water smashing into the tile basin.

Do something, do something, do something, I chanted to myself. A clearer invitation had never been offered. She wanted me in there. Maybe just to see, or maybe to touch, or who knew what.

Right?

I didn't move.

The curtain slid back into place. I heard every soap bubble popping against her body. Steam fogged my eyes as if I was wearing glasses. I imagined every single motion, every drop sliding against her, wanting to be each one.

And I didn't move.

After a couple of lifetimes passed, during which I hardly breathed, the faucet squeaked again and the water stopped rushing. Tiny plops echoed, as if she was wringing the water out of her hair. The curtain slid. Her feet landed gently on the mat. The curtain slid again. The soft, rough sound of a towel rubbing against her skin snaked into my ears.

Do something do something do something . . .

For one brief moment, I saw her bare arm reach for her robe—royal-purple terry cloth—grab it, and pull it away.

I watched her shadow apply a brush to her hair. Short hair, a quick job.

At last she appeared again, hair slicked back and damp, the robe pulled closed and tied off at her waist. I hadn't seen so much of her face before, really. Usually her bangs lay against her cheekbones, framing her features. What is it about girls with wet hair, all pulled back like that, that is so freaking hot?

"Keep yourself busy?" she asked, walking past me to her dresser.

"Yep," I gulped. "Revising my plan for bringing peace to the Middle East. Some, uh, new ideas for getting off fossil fuels . . ."

I babbled on as she opened a drawer and pulled out flannel pajama pants, a baseball jersey T-shirt—two tones of blue—and underwear.

Also blue.

". . . and, uh, education, that's a big one, you know. Improving education through, uh . . ."

She stepped into her clothes, shimmying as she pulled them up beneath her robe. A neat trick that didn't exactly reveal a whole lot, but enough. More than I'd ever expected, anyway. How was she going to get her shirt on, though?

". . . through school vouchers, or maybe tax credits. Um. So, yeah, just working on a couple key issues, you know . . ."

Becky, her back to me, pajama bottoms on now, untied the robe and let it fall to the carpet. Her back was bare, golden, smooth, reflective, resplendent, *Goddammit, what*

174

are you doing to me? I could see three points of her nautical star tattoo. All, somehow, pointing at me from her neck and shoulder like compass needles.

She pulled the baseball jersey on and turned toward me. "Running for office there, Sparky?"

I coughed. "Sure."

"I'd vote for you," she said lazily, and crawled past me to lie down on her bed. On her side, facing me, she half-curled, and pulled a stray pillow to her chest, which she hugged against her. Her eyes closed.

Good thing, too. I didn't want her to see how hard I was panting. Short, shallow breaths like how I imagined a panic attack must feel. I'd never needed a drink of water so much in my entire life.

·   ·   ·   ·   ·

"Tyler?" Becky is saying. "Sparky? Mistah Dahcie? You still there?"

"What? Sorry. Yes." Just thinking about her on that night made me zone out.

"If you don't want to, it's fine. Just say so, man."

I shake my head, trying to focus. While I'm not drunk by any stretch of the imagination, the alcohol *is* still in my body, and it's starting to make my eyes droop.

"Don't want to what? Sorry, I must've had bad reception there for a second. . . ."

"I said if you weren't serious about bringing me ice cream, that's okay. I was joking."

"Did you say that?"

"*You* did, you magnificent doofus. You offered, and I was taking you up on it. But you don't have to, I was totally messing with you."

"No, no, that's cool," I say, eyeing Robby and Justin at the table. I don't like what I see: Robby is whispering to Justin, whose mouth is falling open in shock. They both look at me; Justin shakes his head; Robby shrugs as if to say, *Yeah, I know. It's crazy, right?*

"I can do that," I say to Becky. "If you'll be up."

"I'll be up," Becky says.

"Okay. Maybe twenty minutes? You sure it's okay?"

"I'm sure. Thanks, Tyler."

"No problem. See ya."

I hang up and rub my eyes.

I think about my story.

About Syd being gone.

And I make up my mind. Tonight. It's going to be tonight.

• • • • •

"Becky?" I'd said quietly after about five full minutes in which she made no move, said no word. Just lay curled up on the bed, clutching her pillow.

It didn't bother me, this silence. I listened to each tiny breath in and out of her nose.

"Mmm?" she said, barely more than a squeak.

"Do you want me to go?" I whispered.

". . . Mmm."

Didn't know what that meant.

"I'll just let you sleep," I said, hoping she'd tell me to stay.

She made no sound. She might've already been asleep.

The urge to lean over and kiss her cheek was unbearable, a thousand centipedes coiling in my guts.

But I couldn't do it. Whether I couldn't *make* myself or couldn't *let* myself, I don't know, not to this day.

I got up carefully from the edge of the mattress and walked to her door. My whole body shook. I shut off her overhead light but left the bathroom light on in case maybe she woke up later and needed to see or something. I don't know.

I opened her door as quietly as I could. Her voice stopped me cold.

"Tyler."

". . . Yeah?"

"Thanks."

As if I couldn't have been more confused, that word scrambled what remained of my brains.

"Sure," I said, hoping I didn't sound like an idiot.

"My keys are on the desk."

Indeed they were. The light from her bathroom was plenty to see by.

"You want me to take your car?" I had figured on calling Gabrielle for a ride.

"Mmm. Drive safe. Bring it back whenev."

". . . Okay."

"Night, Tyler."

"Good night," I said, trying to figure out what I should do.

What *could* I do?

I went out, shutting the door behind me. I did want to take Becky's car, mostly to be able to sit and smell that intoxicating vanilla scent. But I'd also have to explain to Mom and Dad why I was driving someone else's car, and without an actual license. Never mind if I got pulled over by the cops. That would be real fun to try to explain.

I hated doing it, but I texted Gabby to come get me.

It occurred to me as I sat on the sidewalk outside Becky's house that for all the sexual things Syd and I had done—things I don't need to describe because I'm sure you can fill in the blanks—for all those escapades, I swear: this, tonight, was the most erotic—

No.

No, that's not the right word at all. It's not inaccurate, but it's not right, either.

Intimate.

It was the most intimate experience of my entire life.

There were a lot of things about that night I couldn't figure out. Still can't, really. But the one that sticks out the most? Her saying "Thanks."

Thanks for what?

Gabby looked confused when she pulled up to the sidewalk.

"Whose house is this?" she asked right away as I climbed into the Honda.

"Becky's."

"*Seriously?* Tyler, what the hell are you doing here? I know you said you were going to hang out, but at her *house?*"

"We were just talking," I said. "It's no big. Relax."

"But this is the chick who—"

"Yes, but it's okay, all right? We're friends."

Gabby snorted. "Whatever, bro," she said. "But you're an asshole."

"So's your face."

nine

· · · · ·

I walk to Robby, who's tossing the empty cups and bottle into a trash can. Justin is staring at me as if in awe.

"Decided to join us again, compadre?" Robby asks. He looks and sounds as sober as I feel.

"I broke up with Sydney."

Justin nods slowly while Robby freezes, eyes bugging, accidentally comical.

"You did? What, just now?" Robby says.

"Right before she left." I sit on the concrete bench. "Actually," I correct myself, "she broke up with me."

Robby sits beside me. "And? How you doing?"

"About her? Fine. I guess. Maybe it's just taking a while to sink in."

Robby waves my comment off. "I don't think so, Ty," he says. "Gotta say, I'm surprised it lasted this long."

"Yeah. Me too."

"So then, who you been on the phone with this whole . . . Oh."

"Yeah."

"What's the deal?"

"I need to get going." I stand up and hold out my hand for my keys.

"Whoa, back the truck up, cowboy," he says. "You invited us out for a party and then spent most of the night chitchatting with your chicks. It's my turn now, bitch."

I'm impatient, itching to get to Becky's, but he's right; once the alcohol was gone, I sort of drifted. That wasn't fair. I sit back down.

"Now," Robby says, kicking back with his elbows on the table behind us, "what is it about Rebecca Webb that's so—"

Justin's knees are bouncing fast, kicking up dust devils at his feet. Without further ado, he bursts out, "You saw her naked?!"

"Whoa, what?"

"I told him about the shower thing," Robby says.

"Naked?!" Justin demands again.

"Stop, no, I didn't see her naked," I say. "Just, you know . . . partial."

"Dude!" Justin shouts. "Partial, full frontal, who cares, she took a shower with you in the room and changed her clothes in front of you and you don't know if she freaking *likes you* or not?"

Robby breaks in before I can respond. "No girl—no *woman*—does something like the shower thing, putting her clothes on like that in front of you, all of it, unless she's ready for you to make a move."

"Okay, yeah," I say, "I kinda wondered that at the time, but—"

"But you *didn't* make a move," Robby says, jabbing a finger at me. "And *that's* why she said thank you."

"Yeah, man," Justin says. "That 'thank you' thing . . . she really said that?"

"Yeah . . ."

"So you were, like, a gentleman," Justin says.

"Yeah, yeah, it was a test," Robby says. "She was ready for you to do something, but she didn't really want you to. Get it?"

". . . Not by a mile."

Robby rubs his forehead. "A girl's not getting naked like that in front of a guy—a straight guy, anyway—without knowing that it's risky. I don't care what kind of 'friends' she says you are. She knew doing that would turn you on, and she wanted to see what you'd do with it. You didn't jump her, so you passed the test."

"And after something like that," Justin says, "you seriously don't think you have a shot with her?"

"I don't know!" I say.

"Bull*shit* you don't know," Robby grumbles.

"What more do you want, man?" Justin asks. "A written invitation?"

"I want . . . ," I say, squinting at the dirt between my feet, "to breathe her in. You know?"

Justin's nose wrinkles. "You wanna *smell* her?"

I can't stop a short laugh. "No—well, yes, but—no, not like that. It's like . . . possession. I want to possess her. I mean, not like a *demon*. And not like *property*. God, I really suck at this."

"Okay, I get it," Robby says. "You want to be a demon who sniffs her."

I punch his shoulder. "Dick."

"But you're still not answering the question. Why *her*?"

"It's—just—everything. I guess."

My friends take this in for a minute. We sit in silence.

"So you're meeting up with her tonight, huh?" Robby says finally.

"Yeah. At her house. I promised her ice cream. She's had a rough night."

Robby frowns and leans forward, putting his elbows on his knees and lacing his fingers. "If that's what you got to do," he says. "But tell me something, Ty. You been going off about this chick for almost three years now. Is it that you just want to do her? Take her for a test drive? Is that it?"

"Not really," I say. "I mean, I wouldn't turn it down, but no. I don't know, dude. It's something else."

"Something Sydney doesn't have," Robby says. "Because you've made it sound like Syd was pretty, uh, generous with you."

True. Sydney wasn't shy.

"My chances of hooking up with Becky are a trillion to one—"

"Never tell me the odds!" Justin cries.

We look at him.

Empire Strikes Back," he says. "Han Solo? Um . . . sorry. Go ahead."

Robby and I take a moment to laugh at Justin's expense before I go on.

"So regardless of what the shower thing was supposed to mean, if it even meant anything, she's been perfectly clear that we're friends, and that's it. Maybe she wanted me to make a move that night, or maybe she didn't think I would because we're only friends, I don't know. And it's . . . it's *not* about sex, it never *was* about sex. You can believe that or not, I don't care. It's something else. Or *more,* I don't know which."

Of course, I don't say out loud, *according to my now ex-girlfriend, my chances of sleeping with her are actually pretty decent.*

The guy part of me, and I don't mean anatomically, wants that to be true. The rest of me sometimes wants to forget everything I know about Becky, because I already know too much.

None of it is recognizable in the story sitting in my car right now.

•   •   •   •   •

On closing night of the one-acts, I ended up going to the cast party at Ross's insistence, since I left the one for *Mockingbird* so fast. And since Becky was going too . . . **well, there it is.**

I'd spent that afternoon before the one-act performances hanging out with Sydney. *And* Gabrielle. I kept waiting for one of them to ambush me about the night before, going to Becky's and all, but they didn't. So naturally, I had to bring it up.

We were kicking back on our patio so Gabby could smoke. It was one of the concessions Mom and Dad made during her whole grounding, or probation, or whatever she and my parents were calling it. She and Syd rocked back and forth on wicker chairs while I paced, and stood still, and paced again, listening to them going off about politics, religion, law. Stupid adult stuff.

"So am I busted or what?" I finally shouted after about two hours of this.

They both stopped rocking and stared at me.

"Busted . . . how?" Sydney asked.

"For the whole Becky thing last night!" It was impossible for me to prevent an image of her changing her clothes from flashing—no, lingering—in my mind even as I spoke.

Syd frowned in such a way that I couldn't tell if she was truly confused or just being a bitch. And, honestly, the bitch thing was pretty unlikely.

"You said there was nothing to worry about, I thought."

"I did! Nothing happened!"

"Yeah, you said nothing would," Sydney said. "So? What's the problem?"

"Are you, like, feeling guilty or bad or assholish, Ty?" Gabrielle asked, blowing a stream of blue smoke at me.

"No! Because there's nothing . . . I mean, she's not . . . No." I crossed my arms, mad at every single woman on planet Earth for not just spitting out whatever they thought.

"Tyler?" Sydney said, with the smallest trace of a smile. "You said I could trust you—"

"Actually, I don't think he said that," Gabby interrupted. "I mean, I do think it was implied, in all fairness. But not stated explicitly."

"You're a peach," I said.

"So's your face."

Sydney smiled at this little exchange before facing me again. "Ty, let me ask you. Did you kiss Becca Webb last night?"

"No!"

"Did you hook up, make out, get nasty, et cetera, et cetera?"

For some reason, this line of questioning calmed me down. Maybe because I could answer honestly. "No," I said.

"Did you want to?" Gabrielle asked, all sly.

I sighed and lifted my hands in helplessness. "I'm sixteen," I said.

That made them both laugh. "See, he's so honest," Sydney said to Gabby. "It's one of the reasons I love him so much."

With that, she got up, gave me a hug and a kiss, and smiled. "I'm going to head out," she said. "Break a leg tonight."

"Thanks," I said, a little taken aback that the drama was already over.

Sydney picked up her purse and slung it over her shoulder. "Have fun at the cast party," she added, and, after saying goodbye to my sister, went into the house.

I was too stunned to say anything. I'd been wondering if I should invite her or not, after what Neapolitan/Danielle had said after the last one. Now I didn't have to wonder.

But I *did* wonder if Sydney knew she could come and was waiting to see if I'd ask.

I decided not to worry about it. She was cool with it, so was I; it was no big deal.

"So you'll pick me up after the cast party?" I asked Gabrielle.

"What?" Gabby said. "Oh, shit, really? She meant *tonight?*"

"Sorry. But yeah."

Gabby frowned mightily, then rolled her eyes. "Okay, you know what? Just take the car."

"What?"

"Sure," she said, waving a hand. "You're a big boy, I trust you."

"Dude, if I get caught—"

"We're both screwed," Gabby said. "So *don't* 'get.' I'm gonna go hang out with my buddy Wade tonight anyway. He can pick me up. And Mom and Dad are doing their date night thing—"

We both made retching sounds in tandem. It was a tradition.

"—so they'll be gone till late. Just don't come home till after they're in bed, and we should be fine."

"Um . . . okay! What're you doing with this guy Wade?"

"Eh. Nothing much. We'll probably go see a movie in the park. *The Princess Bride.*"

"Is that it?"

"Oh, god, Tyler," Gabrielle moaned, snuffing out her cigarette. "I promise I will stay as straight and clean as a whistle, okay? Cripes."

I gave her an exaggerated smile. "Thanks. You're precious."

Which I truly meant, but since she's my sister, I had to make it snarky. You know how it is.

So that's how I came to be driving, with only a learner's permit, by myself to the cast party. Feeling quite cool, badass, and scared half to death.

Becky and I got there at the same time. I grabbed a beer, just to fit in, and felt a little awkward because when

I offered to grab one for Becky, she declined. I wondered if she didn't like me doing it either, so I did little more than sip the thing for about two hours. I intended to drink no more than maybe the neck over the course of the night. I mean, I was already driving illegally as it was. I waited nervously for Becky to break out her pipe, but she didn't. She only snacked on potato chips and wandered around, not really talking to anyone.

I got caught up in a conversation with Matthew Quince, old Atticus himself, of all people. We sat out on the back porch, where I discovered that Matthew had grown up reading Stephen King as well. We got into this protracted debate about which story collection was better, *Night Shift* or *Skeleton Crew*. I argued for *Night Shift* because of the 'Salem's Lot story "One for the Road," which as far as I was concerned was the best vampire story ever written. Matthew fought for *Skeleton Crew* because of "The Mist," which was a pretty tough point to beat. We did agree the film version ruined the story.

After an hour passed like this, us going back and forth, I suddenly felt the urge to bring up him and Becky. I'd lost track of her and didn't see her anywhere nearby. The words came out before I could stop to assess what impact they'd have. I hoped maybe he'd think I was drunk.

"Hey, man, what was up with you and Becky after *Mockingbird*?"

Matthew looked confused. He was also on his fourth beer, though.

"Becca? What're you talking about?"

I held back because now that the question had been asked, I had to wonder if he was completely lying, or totally baffled and maybe drunk. I couldn't tell if he meant to say *Becca* or if he was just slurring *Becky*.

"Backstage," I said. "I heard you guys hooked up after the show." By modifying the fact that *I* saw them, I figured it left me an out. The thought crossed my mind again that maybe, somehow, it hadn't really happened at all and I was clinically insane for having imagined it.

But this time, I saw recognition in his eyes. It was fast, here-then-gone, but it happened.

Matthew leaned back in his chair, more casually than any person who *really* feels casual could ever appear. That's what clinched it for me.

"I don't know what you're talking about," he said.

He was lying. I had no doubt.

The thing was, I hadn't seen them getting cozy before or after that night. It sure as hell didn't look like they were dating, and Becky never talked about him. Never talked about any guys, really.

I took the opportunity to cover my ass. "Yeah, that's kinda what I figured," I said. "It didn't sound right to me."

Matthew said nothing. Took another drink.

It was like a door being slammed shut. I knew the truth; whether or not he knew I knew it, I wasn't sure. Either way, he was definitely done talking about it.

"Well, I'm going to get something else to drink," I said,

getting up from the rocking chair I'd been sitting in. "You want anything?"

"One for the road?" he joked.

"Yeah, right."

"Nah, I'm good, man. Thanks, though."

I headed back inside, throwing away my nearly full bottle on the way. Cast parties weren't like other parties, I'd noticed; there was no music, for one thing, and there were a lot more drugs. The cloying scent of pot made my eyes water, and I'd seen two bags of pills being passed around already.

I looked into every dark corner, searching for Becky, but I didn't see her.

Like, *anywhere*.

I ended up doing a patrol of the whole house and backyard but didn't find her. Pissed that she'd left without telling me, I walked out the front door, figuring I could bitch about it to her on Monday.

I got my keys out and was all ready to go when I saw Ross getting out of his truck, parked down the street a ways. I was about to call out to him, when I saw him struggling with his fly, trying to get it up. His shuffle definitely had a drunken tilt to it. Once he'd jimmied his fly shut, he shuffled off toward the house and went inside. I started to turn and head up the street to my own car.

That's when the truck's passenger door opened and Becky got out, dragging the back of her hand across her mouth.

Click, snap, crash. The meaning of what I'd just seen leaped into my mind with high-def clarity.

I laughed. The sound was sick and purple in my ears. It wasn't a ha-ha funny laugh. More . . . insane.

Becky looked up as she straightened her T-shirt. Our eyes met, as they so often had the past year, and she froze. Hesitated. Gave me a backward nod.

"Hey," she said. I was close enough to see her run her tongue across her teeth, top row, bottom row, then spit into the street. The gesture turned my guts sour.

"How's it going?" she asked. "You hammered or what?"

"Seriously?" I said, feeling a demented smile tearing my face in both directions. *"Seriously,* Becky? It's a joke, right? Some kind of drama department hazing bullshit. Right? Right?"

She didn't move any closer. "I don't know what you're talking about," she said.

The exact phrase Matthew had used on the porch.

"Did you just—" I forced myself not to say any more.

Becky raised an eyebrow. "What."

"Nothing," I said. "You know what? Nothing. It's your life. Whatever."

I walked quickly up the street to my car and—ready for this?—prayed to hear her footsteps on the street, running after me. I wanted her to stop me, demand to know what I'd seen, so I could yell, scream, shout that she was killing me with the easy way she hooked up with people. . . .

When she didn't, I got into Gabby's car and sat gripping

the wheel with both hands. I arched my neck to look in the rearview mirror, where I could see her reflected, still standing by the truck.

I waited. Waited.

Eventually, Becky threw her hands up in the air and stalked back to the house. Like *I* was the impossible one.

I drove home, fighting, I'm only half ashamed to say, tears of betrayal and rage that wanted to explode out of my head.

* * * * *

Robby is waiting patiently for me to continue. Justin, despite his earlier animation, is starting to tip over.

"It's not about sex," I repeat.

"Okay, so?" Robby says.

I stand up. Robby does too.

"I guess I want to help her," I say.

"With what?"

"I'm not sure."

Except I was.

"You got a hero complex?" Robby demands. "Is that it? Ride in on a white horse, save the princess? Man, that never works. Never."

"Well, no, it hasn't so far."

"But she snaps and you come running with ice cream in hand. There's a word for that, you know. Rhymes with 'wussy-pipped.' "

I giggle. The headache I'd felt pinching my head earlier

193

is starting to come back. God, what a bad idea this was. We should've just gone out for pizza, maybe played video games all night or something.

"Know what I'm saying?" Robby pushes.

"Yeah, I get it. Maybe you're right, maybe I am. Thing is, though, man, I tried it the other way. I tried staying away from her. It didn't work. Didn't *take*. At least this way . . ."

Robby crosses his arms, waiting.

"At least this way I know where I stand," I finish.

"That's dog shit."

"It's not all that bad."

"No, I mean, you're *standing* in dog shit, Ty. Look."

And indeed, I am.

"Well . . . *shit*," I say. And we both burst out laughing.

* * * * *

By the Monday morning after the party, I'd made up my mind: there wasn't a damn thing I could do.

Like Matthew before him, Ross barely spoke to Becky, that I ever saw, and his name never came up when she and I hung out.

I didn't understand what she was doing, or why. And I didn't want to know.

Okay, I did, but I didn't want to ask her.

Okay, I wanted to do *that,* too, but it would be useless.

At first I wondered why, in the time I'd spent with the drama department, I hadn't heard more about her . . . activities. Then I realized: I had. Quietly, like background static.

Some girl at the read-through saying "Everyone knows Becca." Ross in the booth saying "stick around" with that shit-eating grin. Other whispers and asides and jokes that I'd sort of heard but dismissed as being for the Cool Kids only.

I was just stupid. That pretty much explained it.

So on Monday, I played Becky's game right back. When she said hi in between classes, I said hi back. This went on for the entire week. The week after that, she asked if I wanted to go to a bookstore with her after school. I said yes. We went. A week later, it was an invitation to get CDs signed by the bassist from Just This Once at a vintage record store. I said yes. We went.

And I continued dating and screwing around with Sydney.

"Hang on," Sydney had said the first time I got her zipper down.

I paused. We were in my room a couple weeks after the cast party. Mom and Dad were on a date night. Gabby was at some lecture at school.

"What?" I breathed. For the record, I did not think about Becky when Syd and I were hooking up. Ever. Whether by accident or design, I don't know, but I kept them completely separate when I was getting together with Syd.

"Not like this," Sydney said, but she made no move to get out from beneath me or block my hand.

"Not like what?"

She laughed.

There are some things a girl should never do in this circumstance. First among them is laugh.

"Not on the floor of your bedroom and hurrying because your parents are coming home soon," Sydney said. "Sorry if that's romantic enough for you, but it's not for me."

I backed up off her and sat down. "What do you want? Candles? Silk sheets? Blue light coming in through the window? What?"

Sydney stopped laughing. She scooted backward and reached for her shirt. "Hey," she snapped. "You don't have to be a jerk."

Ever notice if a guy says "jerk," it comes out kind of wishy-washy, but a girl—man, a girl can make that word a slap. Or a knife.

"Sorry," I said. I wasn't, but that's what you say.

"Wow, *that* was sincere," Syd said. "Jesus, Tyler. Can't we at least talk about it? I'm not Becca Webb, here."

I don't know exactly what my face must've done when she said that. But I know that in all the time I'd spent with Sydney, she'd never looked scared of me. And had never had any reason to. For one moment there, though, she was.

"What's that supposed to mean?" I said.

Outside, I heard the horn on my dad's car beep softly, twice. A polite little reminder they were home now, so whatever we were doing we'd better *not* be doing by the time they got inside. So bonus points to Syd for predicting that one.

Syd pulled on her shirt and stood up. She grabbed her

purse off the floor with a flourish and marched to my door. I made no move to stop her.

Sydney opened my door and took one step into the hall, then stopped and faced me.

"I really, really do want to have sex with you, Ty," she said. And for the first time since we'd started going out, Sydney looked hurt. Her eyes were tight, the corners of her mouth twisted down. She wasn't crying.

Syd paused and shook her head. "But not with both of you."

"What's that—supposed—to mean?" I sputtered, knowing I sounded stupid for repeating myself.

Sydney barked a short, disbelieving laugh. "When you figure it out, let me know," she said. "Then you can—"

"Hello?" Mom called as the kitchen door opened. "We're *home. . . .*"

Sydney didn't even glance down the hall. "Then we'll see," she said. "Talk to you tomorrow."

She walked away, and I heard her greeting my mom like nothing at all had just happened. I sat on my floor, a useless piece of shit, shirtless, a little achy, and tried to tell myself I didn't know what Syd was talking about.

The next day at school, I saw Becky as we passed each other in the hall. I said hi. She said hi back. When I saw Sydney in English, she gave me what I took to be a forgiving but cautious smile. I nodded to her and took my seat, and at lunch, we ate together and talked about theater crap. I paid no attention to Becky, sitting alone at her usual table. With a box of animal crackers. Tossing my trash, I noticed she'd arranged them just like she had the first day of freshman year, with the broken ones off to one side.

This pattern lasted until the end of sophomore year. Syd and I slowly resumed our usual routine of making out, but I didn't try anything more, and she didn't either.

On the last day of school, when my path crossed Becky's, I said, "Have a good summer. Call me if you want." And handed her my cell number. We'd had no real reason to trade numbers before then; our hangout time had been arranged at school, and always the day of. Spontaneous.

Becky said, "I will. You have a good summer too. Keep writing."

"Will do," I said.

And that was it. So I thought.

Two weeks after school let out, while Sydney and her family were in Hawaii, I happened to finish what I thought was the best story I'd ever written. I paced around my room reading it over and over, sometimes aloud, sometimes not. I was so jazzed up by it, I had to share it with someone.

Guess who sprang to mind.

Since I didn't have Becky's email address or phone number—she hadn't called me, so I didn't have hers saved—I decided to risk going to her house. What can I say, I was wearing my Stupid Pants. They always fit.

I'd finally gotten my license that summer, free and clear. Mom let me borrow her car. I pulled up to the sidewalk in front of Becky's house, goggling at the silver Jaguar parked next to Becky's blue Jeep. I assumed the Jaguar was her dad's; only a prick like him could drive a car like that.

I went up to the front door and rang the bell. Chimes sounded deep within the house. A few seconds later, Mr. Webb, dressed business casual with a half-open button-down and mussed hair, opened the door.

"Yes?"

I waited for him to recognize me, but he didn't. I cleared my throat. "Is, uh, Becky home?"

"I don't know," he said, and chuckled.

Didn't know whether or not his kid was home?

"Um," I said. "Well, her . . . her car's in the driveway, so I—"

"Oh, that's not her car."

"Not the Jaguar, the Jeep."

"I know which car. It's not hers. It belongs to her mother."

"Ron!" a woman's voice sang from somewhere in the house. "Just buy whatever it is and come *get* meeee. . . ."

Mr. Webb glanced over his shoulder with a slimy leer, then faced me. "Anything else?"

"I guess . . . if you could . . . just tell her that Tyler stopped by—"

"Yeah, sure. Bye."

He shut the door in my face.

Shaken, and drained of the excitement of being back at Becky's house after such a long hiatus, I started walking to my car.

I heard the door open again behind me. "Tyler?" Becky said.

I stopped. "Hey."

Becky shut the door and came over to me, wearing blue sweatpants and a new Just This Once T-shirt, no shoes. I felt a stab of regret for not recognizing the album cover. I'd need to look it up when I got home. Her toenails were unpainted.

"Did you talk to my dad?" Becky asked.

"In a roundabout way." I was still shaken, and pissed. Even a gold-medalist idiot like me could figure out what he'd been up to. The singsong voice hadn't belonged to Mrs. Webb.

Becky lowered her head. "I'm sorry," she said. "That must've been unpleasant."

"That's not your car?" I said, pointing to the Jeep.

"Sure it is."

"He said it was your mom's."

"She bought it for me. He was out of town, and she was pissed at him about something, so she bought it for me on his credit line."

Because I was so pissy, I snorted, and said, "Huh. Must be nice."

"It really isn't," she said, without so much as a hint of a smile.

Which made me feel bad.

"Did you even get your license yet?" I asked.

"Nope. Neat, huh?"

Her tone said, *No, it's not neat,* so I didn't reply.

"So, what're you doing here?" she asked. At least she didn't sound mad at me for my dumb comment.

"I just finished writing this," I said, showing her the short stack of paper. "I would've called, but I don't have your number. Figured it was worth a shot, see if you were home."

She took the story from me and read the first couple lines. "That's sweet," she said. "Thanks."

And hugged me.

It was the first time she'd ever hugged me, and it blew away my lingering anger at Mr. Webb. It even felt like she held the hug for an extra second or two, but that could've been my imagination. Or wishful thinking.

Either way—she hugged me.

For some stupid reason only my subconscious could've explained, but never would because it hates me, I said, "So, what was all that with Ross at the cast party?"

Her face immediately registered confusion. "Ross?"

"You were in a truck together . . ."

"We were hanging out," she said, lifting a shoulder. "Why?"

"Hanging out or hooking up?"

Becky laughed. The sound aged me backward ten years. "Oh, god, Tyler, please."

Which was about as much of a nonanswer as a human being can give.

"So you didn't hook up," I said.

Becky folded her arms. "Tyler," she said, "you're a funny guy, and I like talking to you, but the truth is, no matter what happened in that truck, it's not any of your business at all. Okay?"

She didn't sound mad. She sounded . . . tired.

And she was waiting for a response.

I thought about all the time I'd essentially lost with her after the Matthew thing. How much more was I prepared to lose now after Ross?

Bottom line, standing there just a few inches from her, having just received a hug that I wanted more than anything in the world, more than any sexual thing Sydney could ever dream up, I opted to try my best to let it all go.

I never really would, not entirely. Maybe over time the memories would fade, but I wasn't about to lose my junior and senior years—years I could spend being Becky's friend, being in her *presence*—to my jealousy.

"Okay," I said. "I'm sorry if I sounded like a dick."

"You didn't," she said. "You *don't*. But I am curious. . . . Why do you want to know so bad?"

I almost laughed at her. How could she not know?

"It's for a story," I said.

Becky smiled. "Ah, research," she said. "I get it. Well, Sparky, write this down: nothing happened that would ever make for a good story."

That made me feel better. At the time. Because I made it mean what I needed it to mean, focused on those first two words: "nothing happened." It didn't occur to me until later that the entire phrase really could go either way.

"So, I'd invite you in," Becky said, "but it's kind of

grotesque in there right now. I'll read your story tonight, though, and give you a call later so you have my number. Is that all right?"

"Sure!" I said.

"Cool," Becky said. "I'll talk to you later, then."

She went back into the house, holding my story. I wished it was the one I really wanted to show her.

ten

$\cdot \quad \cdot \quad \cdot \quad \cdot \quad \cdot$

I scrape my shoe on the concrete slab beneath the picnic table, then find a stick to scrape the dog crap from between the crevices in my soles. Gross.

"Hero types get killed a lot," Robby says as I work. "You know that, right?"

I nod.

"But you're going to keep trying anyway."

"Yep."

"You're a strange and difficult person to deal with, Ty."

"The feeling's mutual."

Robby snorts a smile. "So you never said anything," he

says as I clean my shoe. "Never once just said, 'Hey, Becky, we should go on a date,' anything like that?"

"No. Not yet."

"*Yet*," Robby says. "So there's potential in the future."

"Something like that."

"Well spit it out, girlfriend," Robby says. "C'mon, let's have it."

I rub my shoe in the dirt, check it, rub it again, check it, and decide it's as clean as it's going to get. I lean against the picnic table just as Justin falls over in a dead sleep on the grass. Robby and I both look at him and laugh. Then Robby gestures for me to go on.

"I halfway sort of might've lied to you guys about tonight," I say, shoving my hands in my pockets. It's finally starting to get just a bit chilly.

Robby's expression hardens. If there's one thing we don't do to each other, it's lie.

"Lied about what?"

"The story," I tell him. "The one about the werewolves."

"Yeah? That was a great story, man."

"Thanks. The thing is, it's not the only one I sold."

Robby folds his arms. I turn to face the parking lot, squinting at my car parked there under one of the lights.

"There's another one," I say. "For a literary magazine. It didn't pay anything, nothing like that. I sent it out a long time ago, and most everyone rejected it. I'd almost forgotten about it when I got the letter saying they were going to pub-lish it. I got exactly two copies as payment."

"Still!" Robby goes. "That's something, right? Isn't that a big deal?"

"It is," I say. "Yeah. But it's not my usual stuff like you've read. It's about . . . basically, it's about Becky."

"Oh . . ."

"I mean, it's fiction," I hurry to clarify. "It's entirely made up. But if you or Justin—or Sydney, I guess—if any of you read it, you'd know who I was talking about." I choose not to mention that Sydney *did* read it.

"Damn, dude. You really are jacked up over this chick. I mean, I always knew you liked her or whatever, but you're like . . ."

"Yeah, I'm *like*. Not gonna argue that. So when you ask me about whether or not I was ever going to say anything to Becky, the answer is yes. I think I might do it tonight. Get it over with."

Robby's eyes widen as I push myself off the table and cross my arms. "I'm going to read it to her," I say.

"Wow, Ty," Robby says. "I just got a complete and total stiffy. You romantic little thing, you." He starts laughing.

I glare at him. "What?"

Robby holds up his hands. "No, no! It's what you're good at. I bet no one else ever wrote a story about her that got published in a magazine, right?"

"Probably not . . ."

"Try it," Robby says. "She'll probably throw you down right then and there."

"Yeah, well, I'm not getting my hopes up."

"Whatever," Robby says. "What's the worst that could happen?"

"I have absolutely no clue. So you think I should, then?"

"Ty, man, you don't need my freaking permission."

"No, I know, but do you?"

"I dunno, I mean . . . I want you to be happy. Or at least not miserable." Robby looks out across the park, his expression shifting to become similar to the one he had at the top of the mountain two summers ago. "Thing is? When you talk about her, when you're even thinking about her, I gotta say, you're not much fun to be around."

My head jerks back. "Huh?"

"It's true. Ask Justin. Well, if he was conscious."

"Wait, are you saying—"

"But on the other hand," Robby interrupts, "after you've seen her? After you've hung out with her for a bit? Dude, you're a party. No joke. After you hang out with her, you're even more fun than *me*, if you can believe that."

I laugh, but not because I'm amused. This is news to me. I feel like I'm looking into a mirror, for the first time seeing myself the way my friends see me.

"I thought you guys didn't like her," I say.

"I don't like how you treat Syd because of her," Robby says. "Syd's a cool chick. Hell, I'd ask her out if she wasn't your ex. And Becky . . . you know, not for nothing, but I've heard things about her. . . ."

"Yeah, you're not the only one."

"And you're okay with that?"

"Oh, hell no. No, man, it bugs the crap out of me. But she's my friend."

Robby nods. "Okay. Long as you're not going over there blind."

"Eyes wide shut, brother."

Robby stares at me a moment longer before pulling my keys out from his pocket. He regards me suspiciously. "You sure you're okay to drive?"

"Want me to walk a line or something?"

"Recite the alphabet backward."

"Dude, I couldn't do that if I had a week to prep. I never understood that test."

He flings me the keys. "Yeah, me either." He jerks suddenly, as if he's going to jump me; I twitch into a defensive position. Robby grins.

"All right," he says. "Your reflexes are still there, anyway. How long's it been since you took the last drink?"

"It's past midnight. So two hours or so."

"That'll do," Robby says. "You didn't have that much anyway. Most of it was Captain Hammered, there."

Robby giggles a little, then sighs. "I guess I'd better wake up the bum," he says, moving to stand over Justin. "Or I guess I could leave him here all night."

"That'll learn him," I say, yawning and stretching. My

heartbeat kicks up a notch as I realize it's time. Time to go spill my guts and see what happens.

"You sure you're okay about Sydney?" Robby asks.

"Pretty sure."

"Cool." He leans down and picks Justin up in a fireman carry, as if Justin weighs as much as a throw pillow.

I walk with him to the parking lot. Robby dumps Justin into the backseat of his car and pulls out his keys. "You know it's a dick move to go over there and go all Romeo after breaking up with Syd, right?"

"You just told me to do it."

"I didn't mean ten minutes after dumping Syd."

"She broke up with me."

"Semantics, Ty. Come on."

"Hey, you ever stop to wonder why if I'm such a dick, she didn't break up with me before this?" I ask, a little harsher than I mean to. And once I start, I can't stop. "Everyone knows I like Becky—Sydney knew it this whole time, you guys knew it, the whole world knew it—okay, fine, whatever. But Syd stuck around, Rob! Why am I the asshole now?"

"She loves you, man."

"Yeah, well, I don't love her, okay?"

"That's why you're the asshole."

I stare at the blacktop. Robby flips his keys in his hand. In Robby's car, Justin groans.

"I'm going to go to Becky's house and get this over with," I say at last. "I'm gonna read this story to her and tell her how I feel. *She* will then promptly laugh, or scream, or kick me in the nuts and tell me to leave. Best-case scenario, she says some bullshit like 'You're like a brother to me.' Fine. But it'll be out, and it'll be over, and everyone can just move on. Sydney, me, you guys—god, my freaking *sister*. And then I'll be sad, and listen to sad music, and write a sad story, and just be, you know, *sad*. Because apparently that's what I've been this whole time. One sad sack, right?"

I fall back against my car and cross my arms.

Robby belches. "Okay. Got that outta yer system, Nancy?"

". . . Yes."

"Good. Go do your thing. Lemme know how it goes."

I glance up. "That's it?"

"It's your story. Give it a big finish." Robby isolates his car key on the ring. "I'll see ya later, writer man."

He climbs into the car and drives out of the parking lot. I watch him go, not sure if I'm still pissed or what.

Guess it doesn't matter.

I get into my car and leave the park behind.

I stop at a 7-Eleven to pick up a pint of Chocolate Fudge Brownie for Becky, and head for her house. Upon pulling up to the sidewalk, my usual space, it occurs to me I don't want to ring the bell or knock on the door; it's past one, and her dad's Jag is in the driveway, and I don't want to risk waking him up. Especially if he has a *houseguest*.

Becky solves the problem by opening the front door just as I'm shutting off my lights. She stands there waiting for me, wearing sneakers, jeans, and a fitted black T-shirt outlining the concave curve of her waist. Her hair, which she's let grow the last few months, is pinned back off her face. She gives me a weak wave as I approach.

I have the *LQR* in my hand, and I suddenly don't want to reveal it to her, so I fold it once, remembering how I almost smacked Sydney for doing the same thing, and stuff it into my back pocket while still in shadow so Becky can't see me do it. I walk up to her.

"How's it going?" I say, giving her a hug.

$$\circ \quad \circ \quad \circ \quad \bullet \quad \bullet$$

After her hug last summer, the way was paved for Becky and me to make more physical contact. It wasn't a lot by your usual standards; nothing like what Matthew and Ross got, for instance. But I was allowed to hug her now, and that was awesome.

Sydney and I started to drift apart at that point, too. Quite suddenly we weren't necessarily talking every night on the phone, or going out twice, three times a week. I was ambivalent about the shift, and still too gutless and self-involved to actually call it off. But then, I suppose, so was she.

I made the decision at the start of junior year to go ahead and leap headlong into the drama department as a techie. Ross and Matthew had both graduated, which probably helped.

Becky's star continued to rise as she was cast as the lead actress in the fall play, a comedy called *Sylvia,* in which she played a dog. I know how that probably sounds, but it was actually pretty cool; she had lines like a normal person, but they were all "dog thoughts." I thought she was hysterical.

Apparently, so did everyone else working on the show, because they kept laughing during the rehearsal process. But still, I couldn't help but see that most everyone ignored her *except* for when she was onstage or involved in something directly related to the show, like taking notes after rehearsal or talking to the costume and makeup people. No one was cruel or anything, and they all seemed happy enough to say hello to her and work with her onstage. But beyond that, I saw no other friends besides me. Or boyfriends.

We grew closer as friends during that show. But only as friends. Which hurt in many ways; I sometimes thought about just coming out with it, telling her how I felt and what I wanted, but I couldn't. What I wanted amounted to little more than a kiss. To just feel her lips one time. And not on my forehead.

Maybe she's a terrible kisser, I'd try to tell myself. Maybe if I kissed her once, I'd somehow get over her. God knew I liked kissing Sydney well enough. When I saw her, that is.

After closing night of *Sylvia,* I ventured to ask Becky if her parents had made it to the show.

"No," she said, like it didn't bother her in the least.

Which made me wonder if she'd even told them, so I asked her that, too.

"Ty," she answered, "have you been in my kitchen?"

"Sure."

"Ever see a magnet or photos or anything on the fridge? A shopping list, a menu from Hungry Howie's, anything?"

"No." It was true; their kitchen was immaculate. Un-lived-in.

"I put a poster for the show up there two weeks ago," she said. "A *poster*, Ty. It's still there. Last week I circled my name in the cast list with a black Sharpie. Okay?"

I nodded quickly. I got the message. And my rage at Mr. and Mrs. Webb swelled. Here was this cute, intelligent, talented kid, and they just didn't give a shit? You go to your kid's events. That's common knowledge. You just do. You do, unless you're too wrapped up in your insurance business, or in how much you hate your wife or husband.

I wanted to gently offer this common sense into their minds. With, say, a baseball bat.

"So, are you going to the cast party?" I asked Becky.

"Nah," she said. "Maybe next time."

I was relieved. I didn't need a repeat of certain previous parties.

"Well then, you want to go get a bite to eat or something?" I asked.

"Not tonight," she said. "Maybe tomorrow?"

Damn, I'd thought, and fought hard not to dwell on what she might be doing until then. "Okay, yeah," I said. "Tomorrow's cool."

"Cool. Great job tonight, Sparky."

"You too, Mustardseed."

She gave me a hug. "I ever tell you how much I love when you call me that?"

The defeat I felt at not going out with her that night disappeared. "No, actually," I said, grinning like a fool.

"Well, I do," Becky said. She released me. "I'll call you."

"Cool. Drive safe."

"Oh, you know me," she said, rolling her eyes. She waved and began making her way down the hall. No one else hugged her or congratulated her on the performance.

I watched her go toward the double doors that led outside—and blinked rapidly when I realized she was being followed by this guy Scott, one of the actors. Not closely, but maybe ten feet behind.

When Becky got to the doors, she opened one, then glanced over her shoulder. Scott picked up his pace just a tiny bit. Becky, seeing this, went on through the door. Scott got to it before it latched closed and went after her.

I could have screamed. Instead, I spent as long as possible in the auditorium doing my idiot check, and when I was done, I kept my head down on the way to my car in case they were still out in the parking lot.

On Sunday, Becky called, and we went out to a Mexican food place and talked about TV shows, movies, and Not Scott.

· · · · ·

Standing in her driveway, Becky says, "I don't want to talk about it." She says this as she hugs me. "I want to talk about what's in that plastic sack."

I step back and hold the bag toward her. "Ben and Jerry's, as requested."

"You are made of awesome," she says. "Come on in."

I follow her back to her bedroom, where she shuts the door and sits down at the head of the bed, her back against the headboard. I sit beside her.

"So, you broke up with Syd, huh?" she says, digging in to the ice cream.

"She broke up with me," I say. "Technically."

"Yeah? How are you feeling?"

"Good, mostly," I say, which is true. *Jesus,* I think, *I'm sitting beside the girl of my dreams on her own bed. It isn't the first time, and yet it never, ever gets old. I have no complaints.*

I mean, we could be doing *more* than sitting . . . but whatever.

"How about you?" I ask her.

"Tyler, you worry way too much," she says, taking another bite of her ice cream.

"Sorry," I say. "Just haven't heard you talk like you did tonight on the phone."

"Yeah?" she says around a mouthful of chocolate ice cream. "How'd I talk?"

"Upset."

"You've never heard me upset before?"

"Not like that."

Her mouth stops working, as if the ice cream has frozen her jaw. After a moment, she swallows and puts the carton on her night table. She swaps chewing ice cream for chewing her lip.

"Did I ever tell you that my parents only stayed together because of me?" she asks.

"Yes, actually. A while back. You said your brother told you something along those lines."

"Well, it's true." Her shoulders spasm up and down, a careless shrug.

"How do you know?" I ask, except from the feeling in my gut, I'm pretty sure I have the answer.

"They said it tonight."

Bingo.

"Not long after Mom told me she hated me," Becky goes on. "After Dad came home. We had a bit of a discussion. It was volcanic."

For the most part, I've never known Becky Webb to get overly emotional or melodramatic, so I use a joking tone to cover the truth of what I say next. "I feel like I should put my arm around you now or something."

She turns her head to me. "Why?" Her face is serious.

So much for a joke.

"Because I hate to see you hurt," I say. And then once that's been said, I can't stop the rest: "I hate *them*. Both of them. I hate how they treat you, I hate how they dismiss you. I hate that you put a poster for the last show on your fridge and they ignored it. I hate how they went off about how great Matthew was last year and didn't say one word about you."

Becky's face grows even more serious, more inquisitive.

"You remember that?" she says quietly.

"Yes. I wanted to kneecap them right then and there."

Becky centers her head, appearing to gaze down the bed at her outstretched legs.

"That's . . . ," she begins, then stops. Shakes her head wonderingly.

I sit quietly. She's clearly thinking hard about something. Time drags. I study her star tattoo. The blue in the ink seems vibrant tonight.

"Sometimes," she says at last, "I wish they hit me."

I start to argue this view, but she steamrolls on.

"Or were into drugs," she says, "or were alcoholics. I've tried for years to . . . if there was something I could blame, it might be easier, you know? Instead, they're just genetically predisposed to be assholes."

I risk putting my hand on her leg. Low, near her knee.

"It sucks," I say.

"I'm supposed to be grateful," Becky says, her voice edged. "I'm supposed to be happy they don't do those other things, that they have money. That they're still married, if you can believe that."

"Who says that?"

"My psychiatrist."

I try not to react to that, but the news kind of surprises me. On the other hand, who *hasn't* seen a therapist? More to the point, really: who *shouldn't*?

"That's a pretty messed-up thing for a psychiatrist to say," I tell her.

Becky nods. "Yeah, isn't it? But it *might* be, it just *might* possibly be because he's a golfing buddy of my dad's."

My head juts out from my neck in disbelief. "That's bullshit!" I say. "He can't do that! He can't have a patient who's the kid of one of his friends. That's totally unethical! Hell, maybe it's illegal, for all I know."

"Which is exactly what I said," Becky goes. "On a number of occasions. Including this fine evening."

"Jesus, Becky. You can't get out of it? Out of going to see him?"

"Not if I want dear old Dad to pay for college, I can't. You should see the list of meds I'm supposed to be on, Sparky. He's trying to get me doped up so I don't interfere with his precious job or his precious fucking mistress."

"What are you on, exactly?" I ask tentatively.

"Nothing. I don't take them."

"What about . . . are you still smoking?"

"Nah. I only did it so the drug tests he gave me came back positive."

Which at least clears up what she meant by smoking out only when "they" were looking for it. But it leaves another question.

"Um . . . why did you want the tests to be positive?"

218

"See if it made any difference. It didn't. Mom insisted on it, I guess to factor rehab and defense attorneys into their budget. My brother's had more than one issue with drugs, and . . . damn, Sparky, you are really hung up on this drug thing! You precious prude, you."

"I just worry about you." Which is one way to put it.

Becky's snarky tone drops. "Thanks," she says. She takes another bite of ice cream. "We're all just counting the days till I can get out of here, get out of the way, and we can all go on with the rest of our lives." The bitterness in her voice could pierce concrete.

"So you can . . . I mean, you have the grades to get into a good school?"

"I didn't say a good school," Becky says. "Just out of town. Anywhere. They don't care. I don't care. Maybe a junior college in a former Soviet state. Wherever." She pauses for a moment, glaring at her toes. "Hey, do you like my tat?"

"Your—yeah. I do. It's pretty cool." Cool enough to factor into my *LQR* story, anyway. . . .

Becky contorts her face into a malevolent grin, a supervillain divulging her master plan. "Wanna know what my dad thought when I got it?"

"Oh, man. What?"

Becky drops the villainess act. "Couldn't tell you. They didn't say a thing." She studies her hands. "William did, though. He swung by for a little visit in between rehabs. He saw it, took a good look, and said, 'It won't work.' That was all."

I rub my eyes with my other hand. "God," I say, at a loss for anything else.

"Oh, don't even get me started on him," Becky says with another sick laugh.

"Why the nautical star?" I ask, since we're on the topic and I've always wondered. "What made you choose that?"

"It was the first thing I saw on the wall," Becky says. "Good god, I picked it off the wall. That's how seriously I took getting a tat." She shakes her head. "Stupid," she adds in a whisper.

We sit in silence for a few more minutes. I vaguely wonder if she'll get up to put her ice cream in the freezer for later.

That's when I remember the *Literary Quarterly Review*, folded once and stuffed in my back pocket.

Reading it to her, telling her everything, seems like a terrible idea now. She's got to have so much on her mind, so much going on with her family, it seems selfish to ask her to add me to her list of worries.

So instead of whipping out my story, I ask her, "What can I do? I mean, I know there probably isn't anything, but . . ."

Becky says nothing. She takes a deep breath through her nose, holds it a moment, and lets it out. She slides down the length of the bed, and I move my hand so I don't accidentally touch her somewhere else as she moves. She sits on the edge of her bed, crosses her knee with one foot, and starts unlacing her shoe. Once it's loosened, she flips the shoe into a corner, then switches to the other foot. Her socks are blue, her feet small.

I wonder if she's going to repeat her shower thing. Which would be great.

And then—

Then.

eleven

· · · · ·

Becky lifts her shirt up and over her head, tossing it toward her shoes. Her hands reach behind her back to undo her black bra. She wriggles out of it and drops it to the floor.

"One rule," she says as I try not to let my mouth hang open. "You ever tell anyone about this, it'll never happen again. Got it?"

I have lost forever any power of speech.

Becky stands up and faces me. It's a physical impossibility for me not to gawk at her bare chest.

Her hands move to the button on her jeans, but stop.

"This is a lot easier if you take your clothes off," she says.

She's not smiling, not being sexy, and not kidding. I hardly recognize her voice.

Mechanically, I slide off the bed to one side and pull my shirt off. I step on the heels of my shoes and step out of them. Seeing this, Becky continues to undress in front of me, pulling her jeans down, kicking them into a denim puddle at her feet.

I follow her lead, taking my jeans off. I stop, thumbs hooked into the waistband of my boxers, when she slides her underwear down.

This isn't happening—this really is happening—this can't be happening—it's really happening.

My hands quake at my hips, and tremors vibrate my legs. My breath comes out in tiny, silent gasps. I pull my boxers off as Becky climbs back onto her bed and rolls to one side, opening the drawer in her night table. She pulls out a bottle, squirts something into her hand—

I get on the mattress, on top of the same floral comforter she had the first time I was here. She rolls over again, now on her back, and scoots up a bit, a pillow under her head.

My entire body is shaking now, as if in the throes of frostbite. I crawl my way between her, above her, elbows locked.

I lower my head toward hers, looking straight into her eyes, so deep I can see my own reflection. For the first time, I see little flecks of gold and amber in her irises. Guess I've never been close enough to see them before.

So beautiful.

Becky blinks up at me. "Why are you looking at me like that?"

The volume in her voice startles me. Not yelling, but speaking in an everyday tone of voice, not all whispery and soft like Sydney does. Did.

"Like what?" It's impossible to keep from panting.

"No, I mean . . . at all?"

Not knowing what else to do, how to answer, I bend my head down to, at long last, kiss Becky Webb.

She twists away.

"What—what're you doing?" she says.

". . . Kissing you."

"Why?"

Why? I almost say it right back to her. Why? Why *else?* Isn't it obvious? How can I possibly make it more clear that not only is my single biggest dream in life coming true, but that she is at the center of it?

Becky tilts her head against the pillow. The frown on her face slowly relaxes away, replaced by something else. I don't know what. My arms are starting to shake so bad I'm afraid I'll lose strength and crash into her. Not that this would be totally horrible—

"Wait," Becky says.

So I don't move. I can wait as long as she wants. "Okay," I say. I lick my lips.

I watch Becky's eyes begin to dart all over the place: the window, door, bathroom, my shoulder. Everywhere but my eyes. When her hands land lightly on my ribs, I almost scream.

"Stop."

She says it so softly that it's almost mouthed rather than spoken.

And once again—I almost scream.

"Just—don't kiss me," she says, not meeting my eyes. "Okay?"

Unbidden, I see Matthew. Ross. Scott.

I wonder how many more.

Part of me screams in agony, *Go! Just do it, what are you waiting for, you idiot, go go go!*

Becky's gaze is still turned away from me, her eyes open, absently studying her desk chair. Like she's doing math homework in her head.

"You're beautiful," I say. It just sort of pops out.

One of Becky's eyes twitches. The corners of her mouth turn down, and her lower lip trembles ever so slightly as she looks back at me.

"What?" Becky says.

I stare into her eyes so hard that soon all I can see is the blackness of her pupils. I fall into them.

". . . I love you."

Becky's head twists to one side again, but she keeps her eyes on me, lids narrowing to near slits. She slides to a sitting position, making me shuffle backward. She points shamelessly to my groin.

"*That's* not love," she says. "So you don't get to say that.

Not you. You fucking asshole, don't you say that to me, don't . . ."

Her eyes squeeze tight, breaking our gaze. A soft hiccup escapes her throat.

Then she wraps her arms around her belly and bends at the waist, her legs crossed, until her forehead meets the comforter, her shoulders shaking, soundless, naked. A moment later, a high vibrato sob pours out from her and chills my whole body.

Unthinking now, I scramble off the bed and pull up my boxers. I grab the royal-purple robe from the hook in the bathroom and take it over to her, draping it over her hunched form. Then I sit beside her, crossing my own legs too, and pull her against my body as tightly as I can.

twelve

. . . . .

I say nothing for ten full minutes as I hold Becky in my arms until they are cramped and rigid, but I will not let her go. I feel drops of tears, snot, and spit drip onto my bare ankle, and I don't care. I will not move.

Eventually, she pulls away from me. Slowly. Wraps the robe around herself and scoots to one side. With the bottom edge of the robe, she wipes off her face, which is red and damp.

She picks at the thin white skin of her forearm. I move to face her. I will wait. I will do anything she wants. Leave, hold her again, die, live forever. She has only to speak it.

Which makes her next words a shock to my already spinning head.

"Everyone thinks I'm a slut."

I shake my head quickly. "I don't think that." Which is an embellishment; many times the past couple years, that thought has crossed my mind, but only when I was mad, and I never let myself really believe it.

"Everyone *else* thinks I'm a slut," Becky says.

"What do *you* think?"

She holds her breath for a moment.

"That's way too deep for me right now." She drags one sleeve of the robe beneath her nose and sniffles.

"Okay."

The room gets quiet again. For a long time. I don't care.

"When I was in eighth grade," Becky says quietly, "I was friends with this guy Derek. Knew him from *the club*. We'd gone to school together since kindergarten. And one Saturday, we were at some kid's house for a pool party. He took me into the pool house and asked me if I'd . . . do something. For him."

She raises a shoulder, as if to hide behind it.

"So I did. Stuff I didn't even know the names for back then. I didn't want to do it."

My hands clench. "Do you mean he . . ."

"No," Becky says. "I mean, nothing that would hold up in court. I just didn't say . . ."

She turns to look out her window—or *at* her window, rather, since the curtains are drawn and it's dark outside anyway. The glare of headlights from a passing car slowly brighten and abruptly fade as she stares.

"I never say no."

My stomach relaxes, but then gets *too* relaxed. Loose and full and rumbling. I don't want to hear whatever she's going to say next.

Somehow I have to.

"So, Derek went and told all his asshole buddies," Becky says, sighing. "And they started coming up to me at school. You know. Asking me to do stuff with *them*. So I just did. One of them was in Drama One with me freshman year, and he must have told one of the guys, and it just . . . kept happening."

"Why didn't you say something? Tell them to stop?"

Her head swivels from her window to her closed door, eyes slitting, jaw set. And without a word she says volumes.

You stupid, arrogant pieces of shit, I think, willing the thought to travel into the hall, into her parents' bedroom. Sorry, bedrooms, plural. *You have no idea what you're doing to her, do you?*

"I don't chase anyone down, you know," Becky says suddenly, turning away from her door. "I don't put notches in my headboard. I'm not *always open*."

I wince, recalling Sydney's words from earlier.

"That's what they call me," Becky adds. *"Open for Business Becca.* I don't even go by Becca."

"I know. I hate when people call you that. It doesn't suit you."

"Not like Mustardseed?"

"Not at all like Mustardseed."

"Thanks. You're sweet."

It's a phrase she's used any number of times: *you're sweet.* It always bugged me before. I knew she didn't mean anything by it.

Does she now? I can't tell. Does it matter? I don't know.

Becky sniffles again, then gets up, grabs a tissue from the bathroom, blows her nose, and comes back out, leaning against the bathroom door frame.

"So, I guess this is pretty awkward," she says, rolling her eyes a bit.

Strangely, I find myself smirking back at her. "Maybe."

She takes a step, then stops. "What's that?" she asks, bending down.

Before I can think to stop her, she's plucked the folded magazine from my jeans.

"The Literary Quarterly Review," she reads. "Is your werewolf story in here?"

Here we go. Or have we already gone?

"Not exactly," I say. "A different one."

"Yeah?" She thumbs through the pages.

"Page seventeen," I say. My voice sounds like an echo bouncing down a dark tunnel.

Becky goes to the page and starts reading. I sit back against the headboard, letting my eyes close for a minute. When I open them, Becky's expression is curious.

"This sounds like our school."

"Pretty much. You might want to read the whole thing."
I'm way too out of it to attempt reading it to her.

Becky comes back to her side of the bed, sits, and reads
the entire story all the way through. When she's done, she
closes the magazine. Her fingers curl around the edges,
wrinkling the cover.

"What the hell is this?"

I blink rapidly, trying to catch up to her mood shift. "It's
a story . . . about . . ."

Her fingers graze the star tattoo, a detail I *may* have
included in the story.

"Is this supposed to be me?"

"It's *based* on you. . . ."

Becky throws the magazine. It hits my chest with a
splash, paper-cutting my ribs.

Of all the possible responses I'd ever dreamed of getting after telling Becky how I felt, good and proper, this one
never crossed my mind.

"Becky, what's wrong?"

"What's *wrong*? Shit, *fuck*, Tyler! That isn't me! That
won't ever be me!"

Feeling like the most melodramatic asshole in the
known universe, I can't help but say, "But it could be."

"They'd never let me."

"Who?"

"Anyone. Everyone! This is who I *am* now, I'm stuck
with it, and . . ."

231

She hesitates, then pulls the magazine off my lap. She flips back to the first page of the story.

". . . and it hasn't made any difference."

I stay quiet. Becky thumbs through the story again, not appearing to really read it, but absorbing it all the same.

"Tyler," she says finally, "why the hell didn't you say something before? If this is how you see me, why didn't you say so?"

"I was too scared," I say. "You're one of my best friends. We hung out, we talked . . . I didn't want to risk losing what I had. I thought you'd freak out."

"So that's why you said you loved me?"

"You mean you really didn't know?"

Becky bites her lip. Still, even in this moment: so damn sexy.

"I mean, when Sydney told me to stay out of her way, I kind of wondered," she says. "And when you looked all mad when you saw me and Ross, it crossed my mind, but . . . well, hell, man, you were with Sydney. All the time. You seemed happy. And you were cool with me, and talked to me, and I just figured it was because you were a nice guy. When did this happen?"

"The first day I saw you in the cafeteria. Freshman year. You sure you didn't know? Because according to Sydney, everyone else on the planet did."

"Are you serious?"

"Dead serious. You were reading *Night Shift* and eating

animal crackers. Some of them, anyway, you were sort of separating them. . . ."

I can't help but be amazed at the sudden ease with which this conversation is happening. Maybe it's because in so many ways, physical and otherwise, we just don't have anything to hide. I mean, I'm in my *boxers*.

"God," Becky says. "That's what Sydney was talking about? About staying out of her way?"

"It's, uh, been a bit of a trip," I tell her.

"Yeah," she goes. "I can see how it might be." She reaches for my hand. Hers is soft. "Tyler, I'm sorry . . . you must've thought I was totally leading you on or something."

"Actually, I never thought that," I say. Believe it or not, it's the very first time it's ever occurred to me that she even *could* lead me on. "I was happy we got to be friends."

She withdraws her hand. "Guess that's sort of over with, huh?"

Panic strikes. "No!" I say. "No, hey. I don't want that."

"Look at me," she says, flapping one corner of her robe. "How could you want to hang around me after this?"

I take a deep breath. "I already told you the answer to that a few minutes ago, I think. But I don't want to say it again right now, because honestly, it kind of flipped you out."

"Yeah," she agrees. "Sorry about that."

"I don't mind."

Another silence.

"You should probably go," Becky says. "It's really late."

"Do you want me to?" I ask. "Go, I mean?"

"I don't know. Yes. But only because . . ."

I wait.

"I need to think about some stuff," she finishes. "I've never even dated anyone before. I mean, ever. I've only ever . . ."

She trails off. We both know what she means. But what I'm really interested in is the whole "dated" thing.

"So . . . just to be clear . . . are you saying that we could try it? Um, dating, I mean?"

"I don't know, Ty. I truly do not know."

I consider this. It's not a no, at any rate. Maybe that's enough.

And maybe now's not the time anyway.

As I think about the expression on her face tonight, lying beneath me—think about her face when Matthew was doing his thing to her, the look she gave Scott in the hallway—she wasn't *into* it. Like she said, she *let* people do things to her, didn't stop them, never said no.

I don't want to be with her like that.

Plus, there's Sydney. My recently ex'd girlfriend. Oh, holy hell, I really did screw her over. It's not a news flash, this little epiphany, but now that there's a glimmer of hope with Becky, I don't need to make things worse by showing up at school with a new girlfriend. Even if it is the one I've been dreaming about.

I get off Becky's bed and start pulling my clothes back on. When I'm done, I take a wandering look around her room, not sure what to do next.

"So . . . can I call you tomorrow?" I ask.

"Yes," Becky says quietly.

"All right." I pat my pockets, make sure I have everything. "And I won't say anything," I add. "About . . . anything."

She smiles, her eyes tired. "I know."

I want to hug her again, but I don't. I move toward her door. When my hand falls on the knob, her voice stops me.

"Sparky?"

"Yeah?"

Becky seems to be searching for words. When they come, they sting.

"This . . . didn't mean anything," she says carefully. "What I did. Well, *tried* to do. It wasn't about you. I don't know if I *can* be anything but friends with you. If you're serious about what you said—how you feel—then I have to tell you that right now."

I shock the hell out of myself by saying, "You might change your mind."

"What if I don't?"

"Then that would suck for me," I say. "But I can't not hang out with you. Tried it. It doesn't work."

"What if I hurt you?"

"You already hurt me. No, I'm sorry, I take that back. I already hurt myself. It's okay."

She watches me carefully, and I return her gaze without a flinch. Slowly, she gets up off the bed and comes over to me. Puts her hands on my chest. Leans up.

Kisses me. Once.

Her breath glides over my own, eddies and spins between us. Her lips stun me with their shape, how they blend into mine. I can't stop myself from gently biting her lower lip as she slowly pulls away.

Becky takes a step back, appearing to think over what she just did. Me, I'm floating, my head bouncing around her ceiling like an errant helium party balloon. I can't tell if my heart has stopped or is beating so fast I just can't feel it anymore.

"I've never done that before," she says softly. She gives a short laugh. "My god, Sparky. You were my first kiss."

And, well, the hell with it. I grab the belt of her robe and pull her back, kissing her again. Longer. Not too hard. Not too soft.

Then I let her go. She stares up at me, eyes wide.

"I'll see you tomorrow, Mustardseed," I say.

"Okay," she whispers.

I let myself out, walking softly through the house and closing the front door as gently as possible.

Just as I'm unlocking my car door, I see something shoved beneath the windshield wiper.

The Literary Quarterly Review.

thirteen

· · · · ·

I pull the magazine off the windshield and turn to my story. There's a pink sticky note pasted below the title.

Thought you might want this back. Take care.

The note, written in Sydney's careful script, is signed *Pink Floyd*. With a smiley face.

She gave it back. Didn't destroy it, didn't throw it in my face. Just gave it back.

At first, I'm grateful. Of course I wanted it back.

And, of course, she knew exactly where to find me. The headlights I saw in Becky's window belonged to a certain white Sentra. Suddenly, I'm not quite so grateful. I spend one second being pissed at Sydney, but only one second. After that, I'm just an asshole, plain and simple.

Off to the side, I see Becky's bedroom light go out. I whisper good night and get into my car, dropping the copy of *LQR* on the seat beside me.

"I'm sorry," I say out loud. Mostly to Sydney. I know it's not enough. Even if . . . even when I talk to Sydney again, it won't be enough. But I have to say it anyway.

"I kissed Becky Webb," I say out loud. To see how it sounds. And even though it was what I always wanted, even though it was as sweet as in my dreams, I never wanted it to happen like this.

I held her as she cried.

I say it only in my head. Because I wish now I hadn't needed to. I wish none of this had happened.

My character Becky is gone forever. Burned out of existence just as quickly as if Sydney had set fire to the magazine. Or is it that she never did exist?

I start up the car and drive.

When I get home, I head for my room. Mom and Dad are asleep. Gabrielle's door is open partway, her TV on low, casting the room in gray-blue shadow. She turns her head as I walk past.

"Hey!" Gabby says. I stop, come back, lean against the doorjamb.

"*So?* How's it *going?*" Gabby sings. "What's *up*, where ya *been*, whatcha been *up* to, who you *been* with, what's *happenin'* . . . ?"

"Sydney called you, didn't she."

"Mmm-hmm."

"So now I'm an asshole."

"Maybe not asshole. Idiot, yes."

"I just came from Becky's house."

"Okay, *now* you're an asshole."

"I kissed her."

". . . Oh. So. How'd that go?"

"Awesome. Beautiful. You know what? Everything I ever wanted, I got tonight."

"Uh . . . and what's on *that* little shopping list, hmm?"

"It wasn't like that. Well—okay, it was almost like that, but no. We only kissed. Twice. That's all."

"I don't see you bouncing off any walls or turning any cartwheels, bro."

"We might talk tomorrow," I say, not responding to Gabby's observation. My head is going in too many directions, like thumbing through the pages of a book. "And maybe—maybe we're going to start going out. Or if not tomorrow, soon. Like, boyfriend-girlfriend, you know?"

"Vaguely familiar with the terms, yes."

"I really hurt Sydney," I say. I'm not sure I'm talking to Gabby or myself.

"Yeah. You really did."

"But I don't love her. I mean, I care about her, I do, but I'm not in love with her."

"Oh, well, that's a solid reason to date someone for two years. Idiot. I just say that in case you missed it the first time."

"She's not in love with me, either, Gabby."

"How do you know that?"

"She never said it!"

"*Said?* Are you . . . Wow, Tyler. I just lost all my big-sister cred for not having taught you about women better than that."

I don't reply, because we both know I don't have to.

"So what do I do?" I ask. "About Becky. If—*if*—she wants to go out, that's, like, my dream come true."

"According to the transcript, you said you already got everything you ever wanted."

Right. Did say that. So then . . .

No. Too tired.

"I'm going to bed," I say.

"You're not telling me everything, Ty."

"Not tonight. Maybe tomorrow. It's kind of messy."

"So's your face."

We both smile, and both stop. I stare into middle space. I can sense my sister watching me.

After a moment, I say, "It's not going to work, is it."

"With Becky?"

"Yeah."

Gabrielle presses her lips together and says nothing.

I pull myself away from the doorjamb. "G'night," I say.

"Night, Ty."

I go into my bedroom, shut the door, take off my clothes, and giggle a little at the seemingly distant memory of them piling up on Becky Webb's floor just a little while ago.

And that's all it takes to convince me.

I love Becky Webb. Always have. I think I always will. And she is one of my best friends. Which is why I can't be anything more to her, not now. Not knowing what I know.

Robby was right; riding in on a white horse isn't going to help. But maybe being her friend will.

And that's okay. For now.

I pull on sweatpants and climb shirtless under a single sheet. My head feels like it's the size and weight of the complete works of Shakespeare, heavy and angular, pulling me deep into the pillow.

Drifting into sleep, I remember Becky still has the other copy of the *LQR*.

The magazine with my published story inside.

It starts on page seventeen.

Named after a character in *A Midsummer Night's Dream*.

●　●　●　●　●

It's about a girl.

about the author

· · · · ·

TOM LEVEEN has been involved with live theater as an actor and director since 1988, and was the artistic director and cofounder of two theater companies. Tom is a native of Arizona, where he lives with his wife and son. He is also the author of *Party* and *Zero*. You can visit him at tomleveen.com.